I0780328

THE PEOPLE'S ISLAND

Tim Fitts

SPUYTEN DUYVIL

New York City

Special Thanks to tt, Marc Vincenz, Kelly Falconer, Jeong Mihyun, Kim Nahyun, Caroline Meline, Cameron MacKenzie, and John Wall Barger.

THE PEOPLE'S ISLAND

Tim Fitts

SPUYTEN DUYVIL

New York City

Special Thanks to tt, Marc Vincenz, Kelly Falconer, Jeong Mihyun, Kim Nahyun, Caroline Meline, Cameron MacKenzie, and John Wall Barger.

Library of Congress Control Number: 2024952286

To: Lee, Mujin

I

My dad called him Mr. Kang, even calling him 'Mister' in English, though his real name was Kang Jin. He had no middle name. He was a different kind of fisherman than Abeoji. My father had captained fleets of fishing vessels from the late 60s until the mid-90s and had wielded power over his workers with authoritarian vigor. He had to. Abeoji's vessels sometimes stayed out for three or four weeks at a time, and simple mistakes could risk the lives of the entire crew. Twice my father had split the noses of fishermen who disobeyed him on the open waters. But the fishermen loved him. Even though they had to work through consecutive nights in a row, he only had them working when he knew the catch would be worthy of their efforts. In short, he fished for massive hauls of mackerel, croaker, tuna—nets so full, by the time legions of the fish surfaced the water, the sea life appeared as almost an entire species itself, one fish indistinguishable from the next. I had seen pictures.

Mr. Kang, on the other hand, worked solo before meeting up with Abeoji. After his military service, from my understanding, Kang Jin had spent his twenties prowling beach towns from Namhae to Geoje-do, working part-time at fishing shops and picking up extra shifts on charters, and occasionally he even worked for delivery services, and as a guide, and looked like a normal person. But mostly, he had spent his time alone, perched on rocks and fishing with a single line.

As a teenager, growing up in Busan, Mr. Kang had fished to avoid appearing as a vagrant, loathe to be picked up by the police and forced into labor. When he returned to fishing in his twenties, he discovered that fish took a liking to his advances more than other fishermen, and he could live for weeks at a time on the rocks of Geoje-do living almost solely on fish he caught. By his mid-thirties, he retired from normal life and lived his life fishing. He had made arrangements with a restaurant along the drag in Jisepo that had developed a reputation for serving the fish he had caught. They even placed a caricature drawing of his face on the restaurant sign. Abeoji had once pointed out the sign to me. "He painted that image himself."

"The restaurant owner?" I said.

"Mr. Kang," he said.

"Does he still paint?"

"Who?" Abeoji asked.

"Mr. *Kang*," I said.

"No."

"Why not?"

"He's a fisherman."

The fish this restaurant served had been alive in the wild only hours earlier, hanging about with its friends and cohorts, one of many in a school of fish, talking philosophy and expressing their own views on politics and religion. The restaurant also served homemade rice wine brewed by the grandmother of the proprietor. They always gave Mr. Kang a kettle full of the stuff as a bonus. Eventually, Mr. Kang expanded his venture and provided fish to a number of restaurants from Jangseungpo to Gujora.

To listen to my father and Mr. Kang talk about fishing was like listening to individuals speak both a very familiar yet foreign language. Like eavesdropping on two doctors discussing a surgery that you had never heard about or had even been developed. Rarely did these discussions take place on the fishing charter, where they worked together as a team, and if they did speak on the water, they spoke in low tones and never about the fishing itself. When the two spoke of fishing, however, their voices changed even in timbre. They never yelled or raised their voices, and the undulations of language rolled and lobbed, with spaces and pauses for comprehension and meditation. They spoke *thoughtfully*. Most of the conversations took place at our home in Mangchi, where the two would walk up the outside stairs and sit on our roof, a traditional flat porch where we kept the kimchi pots and hung the laundry, a green waterproof surface with two blue water tanks. In rare instances, the conversations took place in our very kitchen when they suspected that Omoni had gone into town.

The two entered the house, however, at their own risk. My mother hated Mr. Kang. She had forbidden him to step foot on our property. We lived in a traditional brick house along the backstreets of Mangchi, surrounded by pensions and gardens so big they bordered on small farms—soybeans, peppers, sesame plants for leaves, sesame plants for oil, some squares of land completely undeveloped with a couple of goats tied to poles. If any of the Mangchi grandmothers saw Mr. Kang accompany my father into the neighborhood, they shouted in succession to my mother, who either stood on the roof and shouted for them to stay away or walked to the gate with a handheld scythe and threatened them with their lives. But if Abeoji and Mr. Kang could make it to the roof without being spotted, they could sit for hours and swim in glass after glass of soju.

There was one mistake that Mr. Kang had made, which was vocalizing his disdain for the leader who had pulled Korea from the dregs of war and poverty. Mr. Kang hated Park Chung-hee, author of 'the Miracle on the Han.' It had taken only one occasion, and I had been there to see it. All three of them had been in the kitchen eating steamed buns and drinking coffee early one morning before taking a group of baseball players who had driven down to fish the waters of Geoje-do. The money would be good, the fishing felt right, and the players had gotten off to a late start, so my father and his partner sat at the table enjoying breakfast. Omoni had gazed out toward the beach and muttered that she wished their leader had lived to see their prosperity. Not *her* prosperity, but the prosperity of the entire country. Then came a phrase I had heard her mutter for any number of reasons, "No country has ever escaped poverty as quickly as Korea."

Mr. Kang had looked up with his eyebrows raised. I could see it happening in slow motion and was powerless to stop the moment.

"Yeah?" Mr. Kang had said. "And then what? And then he beat up everyone who disagreed with him."

In shock, my mother remained silent. Even watching the exchange caused my bowels to cool. Omoni set her coffee down. Her jaws stopped grinding the steamed bun. Omoni hated the Koreans of the politically left more than even the Japanese or North Koreans, whom she mistrusted, but did not hate. After all, they had been born in the wrong place and had no choice in the matter. Mr. Kang, however, was a grown man who had brooded up his position and accepted it anyway.

I decided the moment would pass. My mother would let it go and allow my father to enjoy his vocation. And

Mr. Kang? He had said his piece, right? Why push it? He had made his point—nothing left to prove. You would think so, but he dug in.

"First of all, that son of a bitch," Mr. Kang said. "He only succeeded because the United States and Japan invested so heavily in us and were determined to show the communists what a jewel democracy was. He crushed unions and worked us to death."

"-He had no choice," Omoni said.

"Had no choice. Of course, he had a choice."

"If it were up to you, our country would be filled with malnourished babies," she said.

"Even the mafia has its sweet side, sugar," Mr. Kang said. "Don't be fooled. Just ask his friends how much they liked him."

"They loved him."

"And if they didn't say so, they disappeared or were murdered. Maybe even hung upside down if they were lucky."

"You have no understanding of gratitude," Omoni said.

"And secondly, wasn't he an officer in the Japanese Imperial Army?"

That was it. Pulled from the table by his collar. Steamed buns to the ground, rolling in every direction. Coffee dripping from the ceiling. Tea glasses smashed. Rice bowls bouncing off the floor. Slaps to the forehead. Slaps to the back. Slaps landing on both Mr. Kang and Abeoji. Curses to ancestry all the way back to the Shilla Dynasty, and then the order levied straight from Omoni's lips. Mr. Kang received his lifetime ban from our household.

II

Mr. Kang fished with artificial lures almost exclusively. His specialty was the gold spoon, which he imported from America. The spoons looked nothing like fish, and they looked nothing like a spoon, but a gold-colored metal object rounded on each side. The spoon bent just enough to spin on the surface of the water, inviting sea trout and bass from below that enjoy feeding off smaller fish lingering about near the surface. The gold spoon allowed all of the effectiveness of fishing to depend on the fisherman. Mr. Kang believed that true anglers fished with spoons. If the fish got bored watching the flashing lure glide along the surface, then you varied the speed with which you reeled, allowing the lure to dip down, then pop up, dip down, pop up, run along the surface, then dip down again. Mr. Kang explained that there were infinite variations to this method, especially when one factored in the behavior of the water at each particular moment, not to mention the position of the sun—or *moon*. But if it was trout that you desired to split open and bake over an open fire, give him twenty minutes and a gold spoon.

Before Abeoji and Mr. Kang had joined forces and started a fishing charter business, as a young child, I had watched Mr. Kang many times from a distance, mostly from the position of the Mangchi Pier, where Mr. Kang sat perched on rocks several hundred meters away. Even after they partnered, I could see Mr. Kang during his days off fishing wherever the fish were biting best, whether it was trout in the summertime or bream in the winter—or even during typhoons. I had never seen anybody cast as far or as elegantly as Mr. Kang. A flick of the wrist, and the lure sailed a high arc, either cutting through the wind or gliding with the breeze (the wind seemed to always play in Mr. Kang's favor). Two or three casts, and Mr. Kang would be suddenly thrust into battle, the rod bent in half, his legs set apart, and a couple minutes later the fish hung from his hook paralyzed in fear and probably awe, then left to spend the rest of its natural life pondering its fate in the bucket. But something else was unique about Mr. Kang. Kang Jin. Half the time, he tossed the fish *back* into the water! I once asked him about this. "Why do you throw the fish back?"

"I can't eat all of them," he said.

"I thought you sold some of the fish to restaurants."

"I can't *sell* all of them either."

"Then fish half of the time," I said.

"Then what would I do?"

"I don't know."

"Me neither," he said.

"I would keep all of them," I said.

"Of course, you would. You're a child," Mr. Kang said, and I felt myself shrink. "Listen, kid. Do you see the other fishermen on the pier?"

"Yeah," I said.

"Do you see the fishermen in Jisepo?"

"Yes."

"Do they throw the fish back?"

"No."

"Have you seen the fish they catch?"

Before I could answer, he said, "The fish they catch aren't even as big as their peckers on a cold day. They catch baitfish, one after the other, and they fill their buckets. They catch baby fish and minnows. And that's if they catch anything at all, which usually isn't the case."

"So?"

"So, they are ruining fishing here on the island. You have to let the fish grow. You have to keep the ones that are the right size. If they are this long," he said, measuring up to his elbow," then they have had enough time to make plenty of babies. "If they are this long," he said, measuring halfway between his elbow and shoulder, "then they are fertilizing eggs, and you need to let them have their fun. Besides, they've got too much mercury anyway, but they are still good for making babies. What a life, right?"

"I guess."

"You guess right," he said. "You keep the ones in between, and you can keep as many as you want, as long as you follow this one rule."

"Every fish has to be that long?"

"It's different for each species, dummy. You have to know the proper ratios for each species."

"How do you remember all of that?"

"All of what?"

"Which fish has to be long or short."

"Listen, kid," Mr. Kang said. "What are we talking about? If you want to fish, then fish. If you don't want to fish, then don't fish. It's up to you. But don't talk too much, you'll scare the fish away."

III

I was twelve years old, enjoying a morning off from the fishing boat, as one of our clients had cancelled due to rain, leaving Abeoji and Mr. Kang the morning to themselves. The rain had slowed by noon, and, in spite of the lifetime ban, from the vantage point of our rooftop porch, I could see Abeoji and Mr. Kang stepping off the 25 Bus and start up towards the house. By the time they opened the front gate, I could hear Omoni step out of the house, and the shouting began.

"It's okay," my father shouted. "Go back inside. We'll drink on the roof."

"How can you sit in the rain?" she yelled.

"It's only rain," Abeoji said.

"Both of you go back into town," she said, and I could see her emerge and walk toward them wielding a bamboo stick.

"Are you going to shoot me from a helicopter?" Mr. Kang shouted.

That set it off. Even my father was no match for a joke about Gwangju. She took a swing and connected with the open metal gate.

Mr. Kang stepped quickly outside of the gate where he had more room to maneuver. "Sister, slow down. Don't be so quick to anger. What did I do to you that makes you so mad? If you kick a stone, you'll hurt your own foot!"

"I don't like your jokes," she said, backing up and holding the bamboo stick in a striking pose.

"You don't like my jokes, or you don't like what my jokes are about?"

"Same thing."

"The world is messy, Sister."

"Because some people make it messy."

"You're angry because I poke fun at the Great Dictator."

My father backed up.

"He was not a dictator," she said.

"He was a dictator, and so was Chun Doo-whan."

"We should be so lucky to have had such leaders. You should be thankful."

"Please. Tell that to the people of Gwangju."

Omoni started towards Mr. Kang again.

"Sister," he said again, "just because I am against torture and raining bullets down on our own discontented citizens, doesn't mean we can't be friends."

"Show me pictures," Omoni said. "Show me pictures of the victims."

"Hey," my father said. "So what if we used excessive force? Everything turned out alright. Are we the only country to have used excessive force? Tell me one country who hasn't gone over the top once in a while."

"Us!" my mother said.

"Us, who?" Mr. Kang said.

"Korea!"

"Lady," Mr. Kang said, "I have friends who cannot walk because of that man. To this day, they cannot walk without a stick."

"That's their problem."

"And I know friends who died in Gwangju. They were no spies."

"Then they were infiltrators."

"They were not infiltrators, either."

"How well did you know them?"

"Listen, Sister," Mr. Kang said. "I don't hate Park Chung-hee. He's rags to riches, just like me. I just hate dictatorships, and once he became a dictator, I lost my taste. But don't worry, I hate democracies, too. You think the people out there are capable of deciding upon a sane leader to establish a natural order?"

"What would you suggest then?" she said.

"Anarchy."

"Get out," she said. "Right now. Hurry."

"That's it," Mr. Kang said. "I don't want to drink where I'm not wanted. Let's go," he said to my father, who remained standing next to my mother. Mr. Kang knew Abeoji could not go along with him. Mr. Kang understood his fate was to go back to Jisepo and drink by himself that afternoon or go home early. For Abeoji to leave with Mr. Kang now would amount to high treason. Suicide. I knew it, Abeoji knew it, Mr. Kang knew it.

Omoni and Abeoji walked inside, and I could see Mr. Kang stroll off down the concrete road, then I walked down the backstairs and into the living room for lunch. My mother prepared a pot of peeled potatoes, which she boiled and topped with salt. She cooked up a plate of pumpkin pancakes and set a fried flounder on the table. She served each of us bowls of sticky rice dotted with kidney beans. The three of us ate in silence, until Abeoji finally asked Omoni why she had to be so mean to Mr. Kang.

"How could I be so mean?"

"Yeah. How could you be so mean? He's a good man."

"Am I the one at fault here?"

"Nobody's at fault. You just believe two different things. He believes Park Chung-hee was a dictator, and you believe he was a president."

"And what do *you* believe?"

"I believe they are all criminals. They are presidents. Leaders. That's what they do. Every one of them. All politicians are a bunch of animals who are only interested in their own point of view who have to occasionally rule in favor of the people in order to create the illusion that they are beneficial to us. They want us to believe we need them. They create a false sense of dependency. And then they let us beat each other up. And sometimes they beat us up, too."

"So, then, you just gang up on me with Mr. Kang."

"No, I just believe that anybody caught up in politics is caught in nonsense. There's no point in it."

"Maybe you should have married Mr. Kang, then."

"Maybe I should have."

"Does he even speak to his parents?" Omoni said.

"They're dead," Abeoji said.

"I wonder why."

The lifetime ban remained.

Abeoji would see Mr. Kang in the morning, though. That was certain. Without Mr. Kang, my father could not survive manning the charter himself. The two formed a perfect team. Abeoji was a born navigator and knew the water better than he knew me. And Mr. Kang was sunk without Abeoji. A master angler, he had no feel for the boat or machinery, and no interest. They had a batch of clients coming in from across the island at Daewoo, and they would be there to deliver the best fishing of these salarymen's lives. It amazed me that Abeoji and Mr. Kang had even attempted to walk inside and share a bottle of soju on the roof, even in the rain. What did they think was going to happen?

IV

The truth was, Omoni needed Mr. Kang as much as she despised him. Behind the scenes, my mother was the mastermind behind the business. When Abeoji and Mr. Kang had decided to go into business together, long before the subject of politics had entered the picture, she had put in for the loan to buy the boat, a thirty-foot fishing vessel. When the money began to pour in, she paid the boat off and even signed Mr. Kang as part-owner. Omoni worked all of the books. Omoni paid the taxes, Omoni paid the licensing fees, the dock fees, and even kept a case of million won Scotch whiskey in a safe just in case one of the clients decided to make some kind of claim of injury. All it took was the delivery of one bottle to make the situation disappear. In fact, it had been Omoni's idea for the two to go into business in the first place. Abeoji had met Mr. Kang after he had retired as a fishing captain, though he had known about Mr. Kang much of his adult life. After a couple of years of Mr. Kang and Abeoji remaining strictly soju tent friends, blowing all of their money on drinks and women, Omoni suggested they start their own business. Men without anything to do were trouble. So, they took city folk out on the waters. Fishing charters. Wednesday through Sunday, they took customers, mostly travelers from Seoul, Daejon or Daegu, out on their boat for fishing adventures. On Mondays and Tuesdays, Abeoji and Mr. Kang took a break from fishing charters, unless a job big enough came in. Most of the tourists were just getting back to work, and business was too slow to bother. Besides, Mr. Kang always said, give the fish a chance to recoup. You can't stay on them *all* the time.

With the two spending all of their time fishing and bringing no money in, Omoni put the whole scheme into action. Ask my mother how much they needed to save each month for fuel, fishing lines, oil, equipment, booze, fees and taxes, and she could tell you while eating a bowl of juk without even looking up. *Itemized.* She contained all of the figures at the ready at the tip of her pre-frontal cortex. A bumbling, panic-stricken housewife on the outside, Omoni understood the flow of finance and most certainly undersold herself in this lifetime. Omoni's true place was in Seoul, cracking skulls and sweeping in mountains of cash on the corporate level, surfing the world of high finance. Ask her about the tides, though, or which kind of fish you cut up for bait, what leader weight to use, and you might as well ask her the meaning of life. No clue.

Mr. Kang, however, knew everything about fishing. A perfect blend of facts and intuition. While most fishermen in the villages might fish for hours at a time without as much as a nibble, Mr. Kang fished with ease, as if he just reached down and pulled up a thirty-centimeter mackerel. Mr. Kang knew, within meters, at which point you were far enough from the land to safely eat fish raw. He scoffed at fishermen cutting up sashimi that they had caught off the dock, and in the same way Omoni could rattle off figures, Mr. Kang could rattle off pathogens and parasites. *Staph. Salmonella. Vibrio parahaemolyticus. Roundworms. Flatworms. Fluke.* (Despite this knowledge, I swear I had witnessed Mr. Kang pull in a fish several hundred meters from the shore, remove the fish from the hook and then eat the fish alive in its entirety, starting with the head all the way down to the tail.)

The moment tourists stepped on the boat, Mr. Kang asked them what they wanted to catch.

"Croaker," the client might say. If the boat ride took twenty minutes to get to the spot where you caught croaker, then twenty-five minutes later they had croakers jerking the line. Or at least, *Mr. Kang* had a croaker fighting for its life, then emerging from the water, bent and paralyzed by fear. The truth was, even if the water boiled in a feeding frenzy, you still had to convince the fish that your bait was the one they wanted to eat, and then you had to know how to handle the line once the fish had taken the lure into its mouth, and then you had to know how to play with the fish, how to let the fish run, tire itself out and tease it into getting in the boat.

"How do you know all this stuff?" I had once asked Mr. Kang.

"Shut up, kid," he had said.

Without Mr. Kang's knowledge, however, Omoni and Abeoji would have been sunk. They would not have lasted two weeks. Did Abeoji, Omoni, or Mr. Kang have any idea of what kind of presence they had on social media? Of course, not! They had no idea that even such a thing existed. I did, however, and what I saw was an ocean of five stars, links to professional fishing sites around South Korea, each praising the team for their acumen and efficiencies. Each review, one after the next, spoke of a man who could catch any fish at any time, and if you wanted to learn how to fish, all you had to do was watch the master. Stranger, they spoke of the patience of the master, how he instructed every phase of fishing, along with the quiet mystery of an elder guiding the entire operation. "Oh my God," was my initial thought. If netizens only knew these men. Two drunks. Interested not in the slightest about their families or customers. All they knew was if the customer wanted a fish, they could deliver the clients to the specific location and provide evidence of the fish's hunger and presence. Abeoji knew seamounts, troughs, oceanic cliffs and the tidal effect on each of these the way musicians carried about knowledge of scales, modes and time signatures, and how you could overlay one atop the other.

In the same fashion Abeoji and Mr. Kang reeled in

fish for the customers, they reeled in cash from the customers, though they saw none of the fees upfront, as Omoni reeled it in over online payment services. On top of that, Omoni knew what to do with the money once it poured in. She invested in mutual funds, insurance bonds, government bonds—she bought land and occasionally new boats for Abeoji and Mr. Kang. She knew which properties to put in whose names to minimize the effects of taxes, money siphoned to the government she loved so passionately or loathed so completely, depending on which five-year term you asked her. As a result of this strategy, everyone in our family was a landowner. In fact, I had learned at one point that I, myself, was the fifth largest landowner in Mangchi.

Foreign tourists were the best. Especially Western tourists. Travelers from America and Canada. These tourists assumed we were poor people and oppressed by our own traditions, working like slaves against our will. In their pity, they tipped us twenty percent on top of the initial fees—sometimes fifty percent. Upon arrival after a day of fishing, Abeoji taped up a Styrofoam carton of fish on dry ice and handed it to the customer, and the foreigners would stuff wads of currency into his hand. My father protested, they insisted, he protested, they insisted, he relented and shoved the wad into his pocket.

The biggest scam of their operation came in the form of catching so many fish that the customers wouldn't know what to do with them. Ice compartments in the hull crawling with octopi, packed with tuna, croaker, bream, rockfish. Abeoji and Mr. Kang would feign anger. "Aye-ssh!" Abeoji would exclaim, as if this waste of life was tantamount to murder, then walk away in disgust, pounding three to five shots of soju unceremoniously from the bow of the fishing boat, sucking his teeth.

"Well," Mr. Kang would say, "we wouldn't have caught this much if we had known you weren't going to take it."

"Throw them back," the customer would say.

"They're dead!" Mr. Kang would say. "How can we throw dead fish back into the water?"

"It's too much for us," they would protest.

"Fine," Abeoji would settle it. For an extra fee, they would take the fish off their hands. The clients shoved more money in their pockets. Minutes after docking, of course, Mr. Kang delivered the fish to his restaurant connections on the drag and pulled in another haul of cash.

"What do you do with all of that money?" I had once asked Abeoji.

"What do you mean?"

"The tip money."

"That's my money. I split it with Mr. Kang."

"Does Omoni know?"

"No," Mr. Kang said. "And she never will."

"Are you a gambler?" I asked Mr. Kang. (Omoni also hated gamblers, for the very same reasons Mr. Kang *gambled*.)

"Of course," Mr. Kang said. "Life is a gamble. You think there is some law out there that requires us to catch fish?"

"No."

"So, it's a gamble then, right?"

"I guess," I said. "But are you a real gambler?"

"Listen, kid. We need things. A man needs his own money. Why are you asking so many questions? Are you one of the authorities?"

Abeoji laughed. "I hope not!"

"Why the inquiry, kid," Mr. Kang said. "Talk less. You're scaring away all of the fish."

The truth is, Omoni needed Mr. Kang, and Mr. Kang needed Omoni to keep the business running. Omoni needed the business to elevate herself from the status of fisherman's wife to business owner. Odd as it seemed, Abeoji was the only person on the boat or in the entire operation with the common sense to know they all needed each other. Liking each other had nothing to do with it. Of course, what do I know? I was only twelve years old.

V

I also worked on the boat with Abeoji and Mr. Kang. My sister, Jin-soo, had it easy. Ten years older than me, she had graduated early from college at Seoul National University and was now living in America, attending medical school in Boston. They had given up on me and school. My grades were so low that it would have taken cram schools and study rooms just to bring me up to average—*maybe* to average. It wasn't that memorizing was difficult for me—the opposite. My brain could soak up any information and be regurgitated at will, but sitting in the classroom drove me crazy. In truth, cram schools would probably have *lowered* my average. (I had once attended a hakwon in Jangseungpo, which is another story altogether, as I was asked to leave after climbing from the third story window and attempting to leap to my freedom.)

My father had a theory that to be successful parents,

all you needed was *one* of your children to shine. As such, they had put all of their resources into Jin-soo, and their gamble had paid off. In their minds, from what I could gather, their job was done, and rather than finding another cram school to be expelled from and taking tests in order to prepare for tests and more tests, my job was to accompany Abeoji on the boat with Mr. Kang, whether I liked it or not. Afterall, they were now going to be the proud parents of a doctor. What could I do to top that?

On the surface, I envied the ease with which the two men worked. Of course, I also felt useless. With Abeoji's understanding of the sea and Mr. Kang a master angler, my tasks included washing the blood off the deck and serving kimbap to the fishermen on deck. I also kept the fish covered with ice, and if one of the clients puked on deck, I washed that off, too. If there was one thing that I was not allowed to do, it was fish. "Why not?" I had asked Abeoji and Mr. Kang, who replied that if the clients saw that the son of a fisherman couldn't fish, how would that make them look?

"I don't know," I said.

"Incompetent," Mr. Kang said. "Besides, you're bad luck."

If one of the clients, however, wanted a beer, I got them a beer. If they wanted makgeolli, I filled the metal teapot and poured them a cup. If the clients were American, or Canadian, and they tipped me a couple thousand won, the money disappeared from my hands before I could stuff it into my pocket.

"We'll take that," Mr. Kang would say, laughing.

"He took my money," I would say to Abeoji.

"Who took what money?"

"The client tipped me, and Mr. Kang took it."

"That's because it's my money," Abeoji would say.

"That's right. That money pays for your ticket on the boat," Mr. Kang said.

"Here," Abeoji said and gave me a 500 won coin. "The rest is your fee."

"Why do I have to pay to get on board?"

"Just like everybody else," Mr. Kang would say.

"You don't have to pay to get on board."

"The hell I don't. I spent half my life learning how to fish. How do you think I learned to do what I do?"

"I don't know."

"That's right, you don't know. Your father spent his life on fishing vessels. You think fishing captains get a normal family life?"

"I don't know."

"They don't. They don't even get to eat and sleep at normal times, and do you know what happens to shitty fishing captains?"

"What?"

"They become fish food. So, you get to mop blood and puke for a while."

"Sounds fun," I said.

"You should try employment in a work farm. I'll give you a hint, they don't pay you there, either."

I regretted even taking the money. I should have called Mr. Kang over to take it for me.

"By the way," Mr. Kang said, "Grab me a Pocari."

I handed him a bottle and he turned around without so much as a thanks. I shouldn't have been surprised. Nothing pleased Mr. Kang.

"Want a jjim-bang, Mr. Kang?"

"*No, they weigh me down.*"

"Rice ball, Kang son-sang-nim?"

"*Not enough kimchi in this one.*"

"How about this one?"

"*Too much rice.*"

"Want a beer?"

"*No. Beer is for customers. We'll get drunk later. You want one?*"

"Sure."

"*Too bad. You're too young.*"

"Just one?"

"*Hey kid,*" Mr. Kang would always say, dropping the humiliation bomb on me, "*Stop talking, you'll scare the fish.*"

Oh, Mr. Kang used this phrase for every occasion. Should we murder a school of mackerel out by the sea shelf, leaving the clientele dumbstruck with joy? The moment I cheered he would look at me and say, "Shut up kid, you'll scare the fish," bringing the house down with laughter. Standing ovations. Applause. *Encore.* With any luck, the customers would chime in and repeat the refrain. "Shut up, kid. You'll scare the fish!" Mr. Kang even taught a group of Americans to say the phrase in Korean. "Yamma, shikkeureo. Mulgogi nollanda."

Upon arrival at the docks, I might exclaim, "What a day!"

"Shut up kid. You'll scare the fish."

"See you tomorrow, Mr. Kang."

"Shut up kid. You'll scare the fish."

"Why do you let Mr. Kang talk to me like that?" I asked my dad once.

"Because you're a kid, and it's a man's job to make sure a kid knows who's boss."

"I *know* who's boss."

"It's his job to keep reminding you, to keep you in line, to wear you down and make you never want to cross him."

"I don't want to cross him *now*."

"Then it looks like he is doing his job."

"What a job."

"Look, son," Abeoji said. "Sometimes it feels good to embarrass other people. Mr. Kang likes it, and he is good at what he does, and I respect that. Our life was much harder than yours. You have no reason to complain. Your life is so easy. When I was a fishing captain, keeping order was a matter of life and death. I used to make some of my fishermen swim home."

"What if they drowned?"

"They probably did drown! That was none of my business. But what is my business is that I fished successfully, and that I provided for the family. Not just our family, but our extended family. The country.

And now we have this business that provides for us as well. Ever thought of that? I doubt it. Have you ever experienced a difficult day in your life?"

"Yes," I said.

"Listen," Abeoji said, "if you let younger people feel like they have a voice, they'll never shut up. You have to make sure children are afraid to speak."

"Yeah, but it doesn't feel good."

"That's your problem."

"I should just stay home, then," I said.

"Ha," Abeoji said. "You don't think I haven't thought about that? You're not *allowed* to stay home. It's either work with us on the boat or you spend your day at a cram school. How would you like that?"

My God, I thought. Cram schools. Chills. *Horror.* I regretted ever bringing up the subject.

"I have an idea," Mr. Kang said to Abeoji, nodding my direction. "Maybe we can skip dinner tonight and drive down to Jangseungpo. There are some fine shops in Jangseungpo. We could pick out a new dress for the kid."

VI

Abeoji's knotsman and mechanic was a man just entering the middle age phase of his life. Abeoji and Mr. Kang always referred to him as Joh-ghee-oh, and I did not find out for months that his actual name was Seong. Much like Mr. Kang, Seong lived a monastic life, other than fishing, Seong spent all of his time off the boat painting. He spent every bit of his fishing money on painting supplies, canvases, and other tools of the trade, and even when he was out on the boat, he wore pants and shirts covered in splotches and streaks of just about every color. Physically, Seong appeared almost feminine, enough to pass as a young woman. His jawline appeared triangular, as if it had already been carved by the plastic surgeon's knife, and his lips seemed to have a shade of lipstick. He drove a sporty hybrid between a motorcycle and bicycle that made a high whiny sound, and he wore a helmet featuring a bull's eye symbol.

Seong, according to his parents and grandparents, had inherited a small island off the coast of Korea, several kilometers from Nambu. We had passed it a number of times, and both Mr. Kang and Seong had pointed it out.

"That's not an island," Mr. Kang said. "It's an islet."

"It's not even an islet," Abeoji said. "Probably a seamount."

"Seamounts don't have trees," Mr. Kang said. "It's an islet."

Either way, Seong's island jutted out of the water with a tuft of forest on top, interwoven with jagged granite stones, weather beaten and raw. On one side of the island, the rocks sliced into the water at just enough of an angle where one might fix a dock, but even still, the island seemed like a sitting duck for typhoons. The word *barren* would not have been inappropriate. Suicide Island might have been a proper name for the place.

Rumor had it than in the depths surrounding Seong's island existed a bed of oysters rich with pearls. Seong said it was probably family lore. "After all, if it were true," he had said, "then somebody would have gone down there looking for them. God knows we needed the money."

"But they could be there," I said.

"They could be," Mr. Kang said. "But they could be anywhere." Mr. Kang said it was probably a lie his grandparents told their neighbors so they wouldn't be considered simple poor people.

"You're probably right," Seong said.

"Which would you rather be," Mr. Kang asked, "a poor person, one step from destitution, or living in utter poverty sitting on a mountain of pearls?"

"Exactly," Seong said. "After all, there were plenty of village folk claiming to be the descendants of Yi Sun-shin, King Sejong, or even Park Chung Hee. Even *Kim Il-sung*."

"There are all types," Mr. Kang said. "Anything to get a step up over your neighbor."

Seong himself hailed from Gwangju, and he even had known uncles who had been killed in the 1980 uprising. Even his father had been beaten brutally by the soldiers. Abeoji knew better than to invite him over to the house. Mr. Kang was bad enough. Seong would have been a double whammy, too much for Omoni to bear, and business owner or not, she might very well bring the whole business down. Why not? Even *former*-business owner had a pretty good ring to it.

I loved Seong's sense of style, and once, I even snuck onto the 67-1 bus to Jangseungpo and bought a bunch of paints to splotch my own clothes, which threw Omoni into a screaming fit, working me over with a bamboo cane. Omoni wept all night that the clothes had been ruined and could never be worn again. Abeoji looked at it differently. "It's not that you have ruined the clothes," he had said. "It's not even that you are dressing like something you're not. It's that you are dressing like a failure. You see, Seong is an imbecile. Seong spends all of his time painting because he is not good at anything else other than working on the boat. But he thinks working on the boat makes him seem low class, so he is trying to be something he isn't."

"Why doesn't he do anything else?"

"He can't. He failed out of school. He failed his college exam. He almost got kicked out of the military for his ineptitude."

"Have you seen his paintings?"

"I have."

"What do they look like?"

"Like a child playing with paint."

"Are they interesting?"

"Do you think they are interesting?"

"Probably."

"If his paintings are so interesting, then why is he working on a fishing boat?"

"I don't know."

"Exactly," Abeoji said. "But he'll grow up soon, and eventually, he will give up on that part of his life completely. And then Abeoji gave *me* a double whammy. He called Omoni into the room and told her that I wanted to fail my college exams, fail out of school and become a nobody. My dream was to become a painter. There was no use running. Once the bamboo stick was in Omoni's hands she could have tried out for the Olympics, and any serious getaway attempt only amplified the beating.

VI

Maybe Abeoji was right. Seong did have a faraway look on his face, and he talked openly about how he was going to move to America one day, and that we would see his paintings in magazines and on the TV news, in galleries, and he would be walking elbow to elbow with famous actors and musicians. We would be telling our friends that we once worked with him, and he was the most down-to-earth person we had ever met. He was just like everybody else. These stories always entertained Mr. Kang, who, should he get chum on his pants or shirt, might turn to Abeoji, and the customers and say, "Hey, remind you of anybody?"

"Hajimata," Abeoji would say, and tell Mr. Kang that Seong was trying, and who knows, lots of crazy people became famous. "Even if he is an imbecile, it's better to try and fail than to have never tried." *What? No bamboo stick? No slaps to the forehead and mouth? No yanking at the earlobes and tears?*

But Seong was not like everybody else. His name fit him, as he often brought along his acoustic guitar and sang versions of American pop songs in Korean. He sang John Denver, "Country Roads." He sang James Taylor, and sometimes he would play transposed Bach partitas. Somehow, this did not enrage my father or Mr. Kang, as for some reason, Seong's music actually *improved* fishing conditions. (This was somewhat of a credit to my father and Mr. Kang's personalities— when something out of the ordinary worked, they never questioned the logic and immediately included it into the process. If banging pots and pans would have attracted fish, they would have banged pots and pans.) For some reason, Seong's voice and playing seemed to hypnotize the fish. Especially mackerel. As such, the two men required Seong to bring his guitar, and they considered the absence of the instrument to be abject bad luck, akin to cursing ancestors or jamming your chopsticks into your rice.

Seong's fingers mesmerized me when he played the guitar. His left hand crawled up and down the neck of the guitar like a different species, one finger lifting, another setting down, while two others remained steady, then in bursts, all of the fingers scattered in different directions. Seong's left hand seemed to barely move at all, and somehow more sounds came out of the guitar than the movement of his hands altogether.

Above all, Seong was a master knotsman. When my father and Mr. Kang showed up at the Jisepo docks, Seong had already been there for at least an hour, arranging leaders tied with knots specific to each fish and lure. For bream and smaller rockfish and trout, he tied Turle knots to small hooks. For attaching monofilament to leaders, he used the clinched knot. Palomar knots Seong tied to larger hooks to bring in the big game, as well as to artificial lures. The blood knot, to me, seemed like the master of all knots, mysterious and against all laws of nature, attaching string to string. Whenever I attempted these knots, the lines tightened, then oozed apart like liquid. With all other knots you could fake it. You would not catch any fish, but you could pretend to know what you were doing. There was no faking the blood knot—the lines just would not stay together.

Naturally, tourists and nearly every customer had no knowledge or feel for artificial lures, so most of them fished with bait, which Seong had already filled inside the tank. Seong had a panel of knots tied to a variety of hooks, depending on the bait, whether it be strips of squid, small fish or shrimp. Naturally, most clientele lacked any understanding of what to do once a fish was on the line. Why they could or could not land a hooked fish puzzled our customers. They lacked any understanding of whether to keep the line tight or loose, depending on the fish, or that fish could snap weaker lines with sheer strength or weight, slice through the line with their gills or even bite straight through the monofilament if their teeth were up to the task. With that in mind, Seong tied three or four times the necessary number of knots and lures so they could easily change leaders once the fish had snapped or cut the line. Depending on the ineptitude of the customers, sometimes Seong would take the rod from the fisher entirely and land it solo, allowing the customer to scoop up the fish with a net in order to still feel involved, handing the rod back as soon as the fish boarded the boat, "What a catch!" he would encourage the customer, beaming in response, in self-glory.

Similar to Seong's approach to guitar, his fingers

moved with an intellectual grace when he tied knots, and no matter how you tried to watch and mimic his technique, it was no use. The visual information clashed with haptic imitation. You tried to memorize the form. You tried to visualize, but even when he slowed down and talked you through it, like a magician. However, essential steps remained invisible. When Seong finished a knot, he pulled the knot to his teeth, snipped the excess free with his canines, then flared a lighter and curled up the loose monofilament into a tiny molten ball. "The art," Seong had told me once, "is to make sure that the fish either fails to see the knot or does not recognize that the knot exists. You see, bait fish in the wild are not followed around by hunks of nylon wherever they go. So, if that knot is present, the predator will pass for a less risky dish. It's simple."

"How do you know what the shape is?" I asked him.

"I don't. I just make the ones I know how to make. If I knew how it worked, I'd probably mess it up. That, or start my own business."

"Stop asking him questions," Mr. Kang said.

"How am I supposed to learn anything?" I asked.

"How am I supposed to learn anything?" Mr. Kang repeated, imitating the sound of a baby talking.

I couldn't help it, but when he did this in front of Seong, I started crying.

"Oh, my God!" Mr. Kang said. "You'll scare the fish."

Later that afternoon, while Mr. Kang and Abeoji were busy with clientele, Seong sat next to me. "Don't worry about Mr. Kang," Seong told me.

"I hate him."

"He's all talk," Seong said. "Besides, your father and Mr. Kang have done a very nice thing for me."

"What's that?"

"You know all the extra money they make with tips and extra fish?"

"Yeah."

"Well, they've taken a chance on me. I traded them my island in exchange for covering the expenses for a month-long exhibition in Seoul."

"You sold them your island? They took advantage of you."

"It's worthless. But with men like that, they can make something of it. Don't worry, I have no use for it."

"But the pearls."

"There could be pearls anywhere," Seong said. "And your father and Mr. Kang have taken a chance on me.

I sold them my island in exchange for a month-long exhibition in Seoul. Those gallery spaces aren't cheap. It's a fair deal."

"He's going to be famous," Abeoji said, overhearing the conversation.

"He's a master," Mr. Kang said. They both smiled at each other.

Blood rose to my face with rage and embarrassment, but by the end of the day, I realized that in the end, they had given him an opportunity. They valued Seong's gift, the songs that lured prized mackerel to the surface, the grace and efficiency of his fingers and knowledge of monofilament, as well as keeping the boat mechanically sound. Seong was just as much a part of the enterprise as Abeoji, Mr. Kang, or Omoni, for that matter. I was the only odd man out, and their teasing of Seong was just part of their routine. They all teased each other. In truth, neither Abeoji nor Mr. Kang could do any of the work that Seong brought to the organization, and they admired him. Truth was, after work, Seong shared a drink with Abeoji and Mr. Kang and didn't even have to look away when he sipped. When Seong expressed concerns about weather, the location of fish, or if adjustments needed to be made in their approach, the two men listened. Somehow, Seong's voice never *scared away the fish.*

Once, even, Mr. Kang had asked Seong, in front of the customers, why Seong wasted all of his time painting, performing the work of bored housewives.

"He's taking a chance," Abeoji said. "It's better than what you're doing, or anybody else, I know. Including me. He may fail, but he's giving it everything he's got."

Later, on the bus ride home, I asked Abeoji why he was taking Seong's island.

"I bought it," Abeoji said.

"Same thing."

"Listen," Abeoji said, "if he fails, I'm going to let him work off the debt. Half the debt. But if he wins, it will be fair and square."

"You think he'll win?"

"Oh my God. *No.* But he will have tried, and when he returns to us as a failure, he will always remember we helped him out. He will be a devoted worker for the rest of his life. Besides, you think I can do this job forever?"

"No."

"Well, someone like Seong can take over and become a business owner."

"I thought I was going to take over," I said.

"You'll have to ask Seong about that when the time comes. Besides," Abeoji said, "you don't have the gift."

VII

The gift. Abeoji's comment sat in my stomach like a tombstone. How could I know if I had the gift or not if I was never allowed to fish? If I so much as walked down to the Mangchi Pier with a rod and reel, my mother took out her bamboo stick, and Abeoji might snap the fishing rod itself in half over his knee. Did either of them have my interest or future in mind? Did they have any plans to send me to America? Did they hire tutors and pay for music lessons like they had with my sister? Did my sister even have any interest in helping me, her brother? Had she ever bothered to call from America from time to time to see if her kid brother was doing okay back in Geoje-do? I don't think so.

"Don't you even think about ending up like your father," Omoni would say, whether Abeoji was in earshot or not.

Abeoji could have cared less if I was fishing—I

knew that he was afraid the weekend fishermen and posers on the pier would have a negative influence on me. In fact, one day, he walked me down to the pier to check out the techniques of these fishermen. Reporting proudly, I told him that I had seen people fishing, traps with crabs and worms on hooks, and bobbers floating atop the water. I saw tetrapods fixed to the sides and front of the pier to keep the waves from smashing into the shore.

"Tell me what you don't see," he said.

"How can I know what I don't see if I can't see it?"

"Just look and report."

I did just that. I walked, gazed and observed. Occasionally, a wave splashed onto the concrete pier itself. The sun began to set behind the mountains, and fishermen with lights pointed their illuminations directly into the water, bringing baitfish to the surface, swimming like magnified sperm on a radiant green background.

"Still no answer," Abeoji said—he himself entertained by pouring paper cup after paper cup from a bottle of Munhak soju he carried with him.

"No," I said.

"If I tell you the answer, then you have failed the test."

"Then I fail," I said, having no idea to the after-effect on my personal freedoms regarding any interaction with fishing itself.

"First of all," he said, there is the obvious answer. "You do not see any fish," and he was right. No matter how many fishermen donned fishing hats and visors, fishing glasses and half-length fishing chairs, not a single vacationer showed any evidence of success! We had been at the pier for over two hours, and not once had we seen a rod even bend in half.

Abeoji and I approached the first fisherman, who had been casting his line out nearly as far as Mr. Kang, but when the fisherman reeled in his line, not only did he reel for speed over technique, but a worm had also been fixed to his hook. A *worm*! "You don't fish with worms in saltwater," Abeoji said, "and if you do fish with worms, it should be to catch baitfish, and if you catch baitfish, then take the worm off and use the baitfish, but if you want to catch baitfish, then dangle it where the baitfish are, instead of casting it out and reeling it in like an idiot. To my horror, Abeoji brought this to the fisherman's attention, pointing his finger at the rod, the baitfish in the water. "Hajima!" he finally barked at the man. "You are setting a bad example to children and other imitators," Abeoji said. "This is an embarrassment!"

The next fisherman let his bobber float on the surface of the water, and from time to time, he used a plastic cup to sling out green artificial chum into the water—not at the point where the bobber floated, but random tosses into the water, as if the fisherman were flavoring the water to make soup. "If you cannot figure out the absurdity of this, then there is really no hope," Abeoji said to me, then explained to the fisherman that casting these chemicals into the water randomly not only attracted the fish *away* from his bait, but the chemicals also trained fish to be attracted to unnatural smells. "Who made these smells anyway?" Abeoji asked the world around him. "Some son of a bitch in a laboratory in Seoul? You should be ashamed of yourself!"

"What's it to you?" one of the fishermen said.

Abeoji told him that he would sooner chum the water with his own blood than use those chemicals.

"Be my guest," the fisherman said, unfolding the

knife and handing the blade to Abeoji, who took the blade by the handle, pressed the edge to the palm of his hand and swiped clean, a line of white appearing, turning red and then dripping a slow stream into the water.

"You're crazy," the man said.

"And you are not a fisherman."

"*Aye-shh!*" the fisherman said, grabbing the blade from my father and returning to his leisure. "Get out of here, you crazy old man."

Abeoji and I continued to walk and observe. Abeoji pointed out the fishermen using lights did not even keep their bait in the light, but in the darkness surrounding the light. "How do these assholes expect to fish?"

"Maybe they don't want to catch any fish," I said.

That was too much for Abeoji. The idea that people might only be out for the rituality of fishing without any sense of practicality, or that they fished because they thought they were supposed to fish—following some kind of vacation playbook—it was too much. Abeoji gasped and seemed to absorb all of the particles of invisible light through his eye sockets, penetrating him deep and sinking into his psyche. The world around

Abeoji was both base and useless. He and I walked home in silence, his hand wrapped in cloth torn from the tail of his t-shirt. We wandered up the concrete streets of Mangchi, myself in confusion and Abeoji in a daze, a daze that he cleared by pouring Munhak into a water glass, instead of his standard shot glass, upon arriving at home. Abeoji loved Munhak soju above all the other brands. Mr. Kang told him once that Jinro soju was subsidized by the government and loaded with mind deadening chemicals. After that, nobody was allowed to bring a bottle of Jinro even near the boat. If they did, he opened the bottle with his teeth and dumped the liquor into the water.

I tried to get ready for bed, but he motioned for me to continue sitting. Eventually, and by this time, it was nearly two o'clock in the morning, and my mind had already drifted to the fishing venture we would have to take in the morning.

"Son," he said, "this is why I need Mr. Kang. If you ask Mr. Kang how to fish, he will not be able to tell you, but all he does is catch fish. When normal people catch a fish, they are stupefied by the result of their efforts. If they catch a rockfish, they have to look up what it is.

Can they eat it? Is it poisonous? Mr. Kang catches the fish he wants to catch. You can be sure that when Mr. Kang approaches the water, all of the fish in the vicinity are on high alert for both terror and pleasure. That is his gift."

VIII

The next morning, by sunrise, the monsoon rains banging out a drumbeat on the roof woke me up. Outside the window it looked as if bowls of water were being poured across the glass. My father was up eating breakfast, a bowl of rice and fresh crab kimchi. I could hear his teeth cracking the shells from across the room. "You're up late," he told me. "Good thing we don't rely on you to run the business."

"It's raining," I said. "Isn't the trip cancelled?"

"Lucky for you."

By noon, the rain showed no signs of slowing, and we would remain landbound until tomorrow morning. That's when the idea hit me. If Abeoji and Mr. Kang would not let me find my gift, I would find it myself. Raining or not, I knew one thing was true. Down at the docks, Seong had already tied the knots, fixed the leaders and gassed the boat. He had stocked the tank filled with bait fish. There was no doubt about that. He had never missed a day yet. Seong prepared for the day no matter what the weather.

I sat in the kitchen, away from my father and ate a bowl of steamed jjimbang with a glass of milk and made up my mind. Who was I going to be? I needed to take stock of things. Was I going to allow my neck to remain under the boots of Abeoji and Mr. Kang forever? Perhaps, but perhaps not. There was one way to answer this question for myself. I decided at that moment that I would take the boat out myself that night—all I needed to do was refill the tank upon arrival.

After breakfast, Abeoji got on the 67-1 bus to Jisepo to get drunk with Mr. Kang. By mid-afternoon, he had returned home and turned in for the night. By sundown, Omoni snored so loud you could hear her sawing over the sound of the contestants and judges on the television. Easy. I grabbed a can of gasoline and lugged it outside to Highway 14 and hitch-hiked all the way to Jisepo. The rains continued, but in steady sheets. I had resigned myself to getting wet anyway, so the water from the sky did not bother me any more than the water in the sea. I climbed upon our boat, untied the ropes, pushed off, and let the lights of the dock slowly recede from my vision, as my stomach turned from hot to cold. This was my chance. If I could pull in a haul of fish, then I would start my own business and crush Abeoji and Mr. Kang. Oh, I would have to bide my time, pay my dues. I could sit on the boat and wash the blood off the deck and serve customers food and beers, but I would pay keen attention to the operation from now on until I could team up myself with somebody like Seong and start off on my own. And I would start off in Jisepo and let them see me eclipse their operation. If I had so many clients that I could not fulfill their needs, I would ask Abeoji and Mr. Kang if they needed any extra business, and I would ask other charters as well. If Abeoji and Mr. Kang wanted the extra business, they would have to pay for it, and I would start pulling in extra money the way they had taught me. That's it. That's all I had to do. I marked this moment down as my greatest achievement to date.

Did I need to go all the way out to Nambu? Of course not. I knew exactly where to go nearby. In fact, Mr. Kang had long ago fixed a light to a stone that hung over the water on an island off Wayhyun. This light required no wires, as a solar shield collected energy all day, and by nighttime, the light shined in the water until morning. Mr. Kang, as such, over months, had trained the big fish to know the exact spot of the idiot bait fish that gorged on insects landing on the surface of illuminated waters. The big ones gorged upon the bait fish, and I would gorge upon them.

I had no fear of getting lost. I knew the coastline well, and the lights of Okpo, Jangseungpo, Majeon, Jisepo, all the way down to Nambu. To the west, a line of lights glowed along the horizon. The lights themselves, appeared as if you could see all the way to Japan, but when you viewed the water from the mountaintop, you could see that the lights were those of vessels, scattered about the sea randomly—fishing vessels, shipping boats and yachts. From hour to hour, the distance between these lights changed, but no matter the individual positions, the lights always glowed along the western horizon. All I knew was to stay between the lights of the vessels and the lights of Geoje, and I would be fine.

I cranked the boat once I had drifted the boat far enough, and in minutes, I arrived at my destination and dropped anchor. If I am lying to you, you can set the book down now, but the monsters that I saw with my own eyes were enough to send electricity through my bones and tendons, ligaments and all. I would be lying if I did not tell you that I wet myself. The taste of adrenaline seared my tongue. There is no way to explain the feeling of seeing fish of this size directly below you and the intensity of the desire to jump into the water and wrestle one with your own bare hands. God knows what I would have done if I had caught one. I settled for rod and reel and prepared for battle, doing just as I was told. Mr. Kang had showed me how some of these fish have teeth lining their throats that rip their prey apart on the way down, and if you get your fingers down there, one clench, and you can forget about it. Some fish had gills sharp as razors and would slice you clean open if you held them wrong. Who cares? All I needed was to get one on board, and I could brain the thing and figure it out later. I clipped on a leader with a golden spoon, slung it in the darkness and slowly dragged the hunk of metal across the surface until it shined in the light. The fish was mine already. My God! The silhouettes cruising seemingly at random caught wind of the golden spoon and made a beeline. A direct attack! Though at the last minute, they veered off. What gives? Second cast. Another monster beelines and makes the same last-second shift. The sons of bitches. Two throws. You don't give up after two throws—you already have action.

I kept at it, the spoon swimming across the top of the light. I shifted my approach, alternating my rhythm, fast-slow-fast-slow, and so on, but still the curiosity and rejection. I added a pause, and still no change in behavior. "Bite the goddamned hook!" I shouted at the fish, who cursed me with their ignorance. I returned to form. Nothing.

Could you guess that these silhouettes now did not even dart towards the bait out of curiosity? They had grown bored with this game. They had sensed something was up. What looked like something was nothing, and now that nothing was nothing, and my adjustments became noise in their otherwise silent and stupid world.

Change gears. I stuck my hand in the bait tank and pulled out a live fish and pressed the hook beneath its spine. In one side, out the other. The fish still had that idiotic look on its face and seemed to know no difference. Fine. I cast this one out and dropped it directly into the middle of the light where I could keep a good eye on it and its predator. There. I grabbed another pole, clipped on a leader with a hook and another baitfish. Same idiot. I chopped this one in half to get some stink in the water, then stuck the hook right into its eyeball. Dropped it into the light. I chopped up two more baitfish into bits, scooped it all up and tossed the meat into the water. That would get them going, and it did! The monsters snapped into form and the bits disappeared in seconds! As did the bait on my own hook—the rod buckling forward, catching on the handle, flipping up into a spasmodic somersault and over the edge, disappearing into the water.

And then something happened that I did not expect. The light went out. I had overheard Abeoji and Mr. Kang brag to every client over the past two years about this solar lamp, this new wave of technology, and how the light shines until dawn. *Nonsense.*

The second rod buckled, and I could hear the rod dancing around the boat, but it was too dark, and fumbling around the boat in pitch black, suddenly the boat seemed like a jungle of plexi-glass corners and aluminum bars. The rod knocked and knocked, but all I could do was thrash about trying to find some connection between sound and object before the telltale splash outside the boat.

There are moments when regret sets in, and there are moments when you can still taste the possibility of success. I decided in the darkness that I could blame the missing rods on the previous clients if the subject came up. I pulled up the anchor and cranked the motor. I cranked the motor again, and a third time, and then I remembered Seong say something once about how you can flood these engines. How can you flood an engine? What does that even mean? The boat was already on the water, and weren't they always flooded? Had the rain flooded the engine, and how did it even work? How had the engine responded with such an immediate and affectionate purr at the onset of the trip? All I remembered was that Seong said you had to wait ten or fifteen minutes until trying again, so I gave it a couple more cranks until I knew I had flooded it good. Just wait. Just watch the stars and wait.

IX

With no rain clouds covering the moon and no watch on my wrist, I waited out ten minutes in the cabin below deck. I first tried counting the intervals between waves but counting waves while jostling in the waves made me seasick. If I got truly seasick, I could forget about it. Game over. Instead, I sang songs, humming through the intro and singing the lyrics in my head. Assuming you sing songs faster in your mind than in real life, I gave two minutes and thirty seconds per song. Four songs equaled ten minutes, but four is an unlucky number, so I evened it out at five. Five songs, then head up to the deck, pull the crank, flood the engine, return to the cabin, five songs, pull crank, flood engine, repeat. I needed a better plan.

This was all Mr. Kang's fault. "Shut up kid, you'll scare the fish." It was Abeoji's fault for working with Mr. Kang. Fine, the man could fish, but why did he have to be such a jerk? Mr. Kang, a know-it-all and son of a bitch. If he were not a son of a bitch, then why wasn't he married? Why didn't he have his own kids to bully? Because nobody liked him except my dad, and my dad specialized in liking unlikable people. How about letting me figure out how to fish on the boat? How about teaching me how to drive the boat or at least even letting me start the boat so I could get out of jams, such as the present?

The sound of the rain on the deck above began with the timbre of sweet potatoes frying in hot oil, then turned into an immediate assault of drumbeats, as if the whole bay itself had suddenly equipped itself with an army of drummers, all locked in and hammering away. I climbed back upstairs and made up my mind. The rain came down so hard I could not even see the lights of the fishing vessels on the horizon—not even the orange glow dome polluting the night sky. I would crank the boat as hard as I could, crank it spinning my torso and start it. There could be no other alternative. Pull the crank, start the soupy drumroll, steer the boat home, tie it up, and when Seong reported the fishing poles missing, I would go on ignoring and being ignored as usual.

I returned downstairs to wait another ten minutes, and water had already begun pouring down below from the rains. Try again counting wave intervals, get dizzy. Sing songs in my head one through five. Had it been ten minutes? Sing two more, just in case. When I emerged from the cabin, the boat had caught a current, as the tide was coming in strong with the rains and wind. I could tell by the lights of the beach and strip, the current had taken me into the bay at Gujora. The Pacific Ocean was literally pouring water into the bay, and to break up the waves and keep the beach from washing away, a tetrapod barrier had been constructed in the middle of the waterway. Guess whose boat was streaming directly toward the tetrapods? The standalone pier stretched ten boat lengths minimum, the tetrapods protruding from the water like teeth from the underworld, the current pushing me closer to smashing into the concrete.

Would you believe me if I told you that in the reflection of the lights from the tetrapod barrier, the unturned key sparkled next to the steering wheel? Son of a bitch! I had not turned the engine into starting position. I had been cranking the engine *cold*. Blood boiling of shame rose beneath my skin and turned my bowels into a hot bath. I turned the key and cranked the boat. She sang. She sang like a jazz drummer stumbling into a drum roll, just about to turn his feigned clumsiness into a sheet of paper tearing down the middle. Cam notes. Hydro-resonation. The boat leapt forward, rising out of the water like some kind of ancient Roman war horse ready to pound its hooves into the chest of its enemy, and it did—the boat rose in the air, throwing me backwards, leaping nearly to the surface of the water and landing square on top of a concrete tetrapod, which halted my war horse in stride, sending me forward, up and over the edge of the boat into the interlocked mass of concrete tetrapods, where by grace of only a higher power did I not get thrown into the underworld of those massive objects, where I would have undoubtedly perished.

But the gods did not let me off that easy. The top half of my body had become wedged into one of the openings, and upside-down, my chest, shoulders and head fixed snuggly below the surface of the water.

X

Stuck upside down in the tetrapods, the first thought to occur was to commit, at the very least, the easiest form of suicide, but my hands had no access to the pockets of my jeans to reach my fishing knife. That would have been easy. Quick jab to the throat, stink up the water and be gone. I would not dare to calculate the amount of time it took me to consider each form of suicide, but all told, I imagine it took one or two seconds. The impracticality of this, however, led me to consider escape, find some way to pull myself all the way through the water, rather than out. In this manner, I could reverse position and press myself with my legs through the opening and swim to safety. No chance. The fitting too snug. Back to suicide. I could ram my head into the concrete and knock myself out, but I was doing that anyway with the waves and jostling, and I had not enough room to swing proper momentum to actually knock myself unconscious. I could scream, but I was already screaming.

Lastly, I decided to take it like a man. Time to grow up. Time to recognize one's limitations and confront them on your own, solo, like Seong, Abeoji and even Mr. Kang. Live and die on your own terms. That's right, time to open my mouth and breathe in a lungful and shut the system down. After all, my parents did not want me around, Omoni hated Abeoji and still she sent me to be with him on the boat every day—on the boat with a man whom she hated dearly and considered repulsive and traitorous. How did she think I was going to grow up with that kind of influence? Besides, they were already on the verge of striking it rich, their daughter on the verge of becoming a medical doctor in America. Chances were high that Omoni had already finished grieving over me. Abeoji would have one less mouth to feed and less guilt of failing as a father. I felt a little bad for Seong, but to be honest, I didn't know Seong. Sure, I liked his style and personality, and he let me eat lunch with him, and he called me troublemaker, but it was all in jest, though I knew he had in his mind a way out, and when that way out came, he would take that way and never think about us another moment for the rest of his life. I did not consider this unsentimental or callous of Seong, but he knew this phase was a temporary phase and nothing to hold onto. Who could blame him?

So, I did it. I took that breath, though taking this breath is not as easy as it looks or sounds, and my lungs heartily rejected the saltwater, but of course, once the saltwater expelled from my system, the vacuum only sucked in more water, and peace did drift into my body as I began to be filled with more death than life. Would you believe that during this process it feels like the exact opposite of dying? In this moment, if felt as if I were being filled with life instead of death! I even felt myself leave the water altogether. I could see the surface of the water with my own eyes, the protrusion of the tetrapod and concrete slab of the platform, until my head cracked again on the concrete, and what felt like feet stamping on my chest, the bend and rebound of my very own ribcage. My God—enough is enough! Did I vomit blood or more water? A taste of soju and dried squid on my mouth, mixed with sewage and rot. All of it pressed against my mouth and almost instantly the rains washed everything pure. I was alive. The rain also masked how much blood ran down from my face and head, and the image of Mr. Kang himself took shape in front of my face, and the words he screamed failed to register in my ears until an open hand struck me across the face, and the incalculability of time applied also to the amount of time I spent weeping with my head in my hands.

XI

I sat with Mr. Kang until the rain slowed back into steady sheets. I did not even look up until then. I tried revising and reviewing what I could say, thinking of some kind of tale that might justify me out with the boat in a near typhoon, solo, and ramming it into a mess of tetrapods, but my creative forces refused to ignite. When I did look up, I saw something more surprising than the sinking fishing boat thirty meters from the platform. Mr. Kang was *fishing*.

"What are you doing?" I said to Mr. Kang.

"Fishing."

"Why are you out here?"

"To *fish*."

"But the storm."

"I know."

"Why are you fishing in a storm?"

"I'm always fishing. I fish by the tides and location, and the weather, too. Especially in a storm."

"Why?"

"Fishing is better in a storm."

"But why are you out here on the pier, with your boat?"

"You're out here with the boat," he said.

"I know. But why are you out here, too?"

"To fish. I love to fish here during storms. Peace and quiet. Nothing but the rain and storm clouds. Wind and waves. The storm surge brings the water right up to you. Damn lucky for you."

"Right."

"The hell it isn't. You'd be dead. The question is, why are *you* out here?"

I suspected he knew I was going to answer eventually, but after a few minutes of silence, he said, "You know, when I saw you crash and your legs sticking out of the tetrapods, I had a monster on the line. A once-every-five-years fish. The kind of fish you dream about."

"Sorry."

"Sorry, nothing. You know how many fish I've caught out here?"

"How many?"

"Many."

"What did you do?"

"I let it go," he said, pausing to reel the spoon out of the water, sling it back out into the black. "Don't worry about it. I've caught king mackerel, grouper, yes, grouper, shark, even a baby porpoise out here, but you know what the best fish is?"

"What?" I said.

"The *next* one. The next one is the best fish."

Mr. Kang reeled the line in, hooked the spoon to the reel and set the rod down on the concrete surface. "Stand up," he said, and I stood next to him for several minutes.

"Listen," Mr. Kang said. "What has happened has happened. You have to be honest with me, or there will be real trouble. You understand?"

"Yes," I said.

Mr. Kang held his cell phone out in front of me as if to imply that authorities could be called whenever he wished. "Why did you do it?"

"Do what?"

"Steal the boat. Don't be a punk with me."

Mr. Kang picked up a second pole, reached into the bucket, grabbed a fish, fifteen centimeters long, sank a hook through the tail muscle, the fish's fins suddenly erect and tense. He handed the pole to me, and to my surprise, a meter from the bait—a bobber.

"I thought you only use spoons," I said.

"This isn't for me," he said, handing me the pole. "Now cast your line out, and tell me, man to man, what the hell happened."

I did as he said, casting the line high, catching the wind and landing two meters from the tetrapod. A dud.

"Why doesn't Abeoji let me do anything?"

"He does."

"No, he doesn't."

"Are you alive? He lets you eat, wear clothes, wear shoes, accompany us on the boat. Doesn't he even give you money for working on the boat?"

"A little."

"That's a yes."

"Barely."

"And that's a lot. When I was your age, boys ran around and got into trouble. They got into trouble, and they got picked up. They got picked up and they got sent to work. Real work. Boys camps. No pay. Everybody's a bully."

"But Abeoji never lets me fish."

"Because you are no good at it," he nodded at the bobber that was now threatening to tangle in the tetrapods and clinging barnacles.

"He doesn't let me drive the boat."

"You just crashed the boat."

"How am I supposed to get good at anything?"

"By watching. By asking questions. By taking some of that money he gives you and buying a rod and reel, walking down to the beach and fishing by yourself."

"He doesn't give me enough money for a good rod and reel."

"I didn't have a rod most of my life!" he said. "Grab a piece of bamboo. When I fished with bait, and sometimes still do, believe it or not, I prefer bamboo, but these assholes we take on the boat would take us for yokels if we fished with bamboo."

"Where can I get bamboo?"

Incredulous, Mr. Kang pointed to the woods. "Anywhere!" he said. He pointed to the forests across the highway from Gujora. "You have to figure these things out on your own. Buy some line. Catch some fish. Build a fire on the beach and cook the fish. *Clean* the fish. Bring fish home and let your father see that you are gaining ground on him, let him know that he better watch his step. But you don't get good by stealing boats."

"Abeoji is going to kill me."

"Maybe," Mr. Kang said, casting his line out again. "Listen. We don't figure these things out on our own. Somebody has to tell you. Now, I've told you. If you want to fish, now you know what to do. But if you don't want to fish, do something else. Who cares?"

"What about the boat?"

"I've got good news for you. The boat is insured. Thank your mother for that."

"Okay."

"Okay, nothing. Do not thank your mother. Do not mention this to your mother or father. If you crashed the boat, the insurance claim is void. Your mother insured the boat, and in the morning, I will call the authorities and let them know the boat is missing. We'll file a claim and get a new boat. After all, someone did steal the boat. I would ask you if you need to go to the hospital, but they'll ask questions."

"Thanks."

"Listen. You want to grow up—time to grow up. You

snuck out of the house, you can sneak back in. They ask you how you got bruised, tell them you drank a bottle of Munhak and fell down. You'll get a beating, but take your beating like a man and be done with it."

We stepped into his dingy, and he dropped me off at the Gujora docks.

When I stepped off the boat and started to walk home, he said, "Hey, kid. Did you even catch anything out there?"

"No," I said.

"Didn't think so."

He lowered the motor into the water and was off.

I ran home.

Sure, I would get a beating. First from my mother, which was worse, since she knew no boundaries and never really understood the pain of getting beat with bamboo. My father would be easy. I'd take a shot to the jaw, maybe suffer a few body blows, and that would be it. But the thought occurred to me all the way to our home in Mangchi. If all you had to do to get a new boat was to crash the old boat, why didn't people do this all the time?

XII

Fortunately, the rains lasted all week, low flying clouds crawled across the bay, sneaking onto the land appearing as dragons. The air so thick with moisture, clouds formed atop the mountains overlooking Hakdong, creating a white cap that remained all day long. The sky blued and winds swept the neighborhoods free of clouds, and then a broad white line formed on the horizon and grew until it moved in and started up the monsoon rains all over again. I'm sure Mr. Kang made more money fishing the shore than had he gone out on the charter, taking advantage of the feeding frenzies the drop in barometric pressure brought about. Besides, I got the feeling Mr. Kang never cared about how the day turned out. Rain? Fish. Sun? Fish. Overcast? Fish. Freezing? Fish.

By the time the weather relented, the new boat had arrived—the same boat I had sunk, but a new model.

I had never seen my father so happy, walking along the dock, running his fingers along the plexiglass, eyeballing the engine. The deliveryman showed my father all of the special features. Abeoji shouted to Mr. Kang, "This one has radar?"

"The old one had radar."

"Sonar, too."

"The old one had sonar, too!"

"Oh, my God," Abeoji said with such lust. It was almost as if he had been delivered a new wife—all beauty and none of the kinks and fusses yet risen to the surface—three years of pleasure until the nag set in. "She's a marvel," my father said.

"It's the same boat," Mr. Kang said, winking at me.

Abeoji even poured a glass of morning soju and dumped it into the water. "To the prince who stole our monstrosity and delivered us this angel!" He filled the soju glasses for himself, Mr. Kang and even me. He drank first, then I shot mine down - my first taste of soju, which felt as a fistful of razors streaming down my throat and chemical sweet aftertaste.

And then it suddenly occurred to my father that something was missing. He perked up. "Where's Seong?"

Mr. Kang raised his eyebrows.

"The boat have enough fuel?"

Mr. Kang checked, "It does."

"We got no knots," my dad said. "We got no baitfish. No beer. When are the clients set to arrive?"

"I don't know," Mr. Kang said. "Ten minutes?"

"Hurry!" Abeoji shouted.

Immediately, we thrust ourselves into action. Mr. Kang and Abeoji tying knots, turning strands of monofilament, guiding single threads into loops, then twisting, twisting, twisting, then tangling, then twisting, then cursing, then drinking, then twisting, twisting, repeat.

They gave me a cast net to catch new bait fish, but as soon as I raised my hands to toss the net in the water, the minnows split. They wanted none of the action.

The ajushee arrived, all three of them. Thank God— already drunk. Feed them some rice, feed them more beer. Give me a hundred thousand won, run to the store, buy a mess of leader already hooked up, snip off the doodads and trinkets, go back and get plain leader with only hooks. They were out. Go to the next shop. Not open. Next shop. Out. Next shop, buy them out. Return to the docks—still no baitfish. Risk the business, go back to the bait shop, buy boxes of worms. Mr. Kang, Abeoji, faces lowered in abject humiliation, reeling in one baitfish after the next. Anybody want more beer? Who's drinking beer? Soju? Munhak?

Of course, on the water, Mr. Kang killed it. Abeoji killed it, too, each fishing with their own rigs, tossing their catches into the box of ice and ready to bag for their departure.

"Sorry you didn't catch any," Mr. Kang told each of the businessmen, "but your friends brought in a haul!" Each of them believing that they were the only ones to fail in catching any fish. "But you're good luck! We should bring you aboard every time!" Mr. Kang laid it on thick. I knew as much to never bring this up.

We took pictures of the businessmen individually, two by two, then all three. We finished the day an inch from collapse, surfing the wave of desperation. "A damn close call," Mr. Kang said.

"Son of a bitch," Mr. Kang said as we collapsed on the Plexiglass bench, ready to wash out the boat and sell the extra fish to the restaurant. Mr. Kang sat up, poured a glass of soju. "Here's to Seong," he said. "May I break every one of your fingers when I see you."

"I don't think so," Abeoji said.

"Yeah, he abandoned you," I said.

"Something good happened to Seong," Abeoji said.

"You don't think," Mr. Kang said.

"I do," Abeoji said.

"You may have a point," Mr. Kang said. "That little prick. When his life is miserable, he is with us. He would never miss a day unless something great has happened."

XIII

During the following days, Abeoji and Mr. Kang could not have failed worse. On days when they had given up completely on tying enough knots for the trip, choosing rather to buy the leaders from local fishing shops, they would forget to gas the boat. On days they departed with a group of businessmen with all of the proper gear and fuel, they had neglected to catch any baitfish. When they had netted proper baitfish, they had forgotten the beer. To remedy their wounded spirits, they crawled inside bottles of Munhak, spent their evenings bragging to soju tent skanks, then crawling back to the docks hungover and sometimes sleepless. On a few nights, I had to go to the soju tents myself and force my father to come home, and he and Mr. Kang would be half asleep, their arms around two women. It was always the same two women, and the short woman had a gold tooth, and black tar caked between the rest of her teeth from years of smoking.

What did I care? I didn't. I couldn't have cared less. Let the business fail! Mr. Kang and Abeoji became conmen and charlatans. With one wheel missing, we were no better than the hacks out in the bay dragging the bottom of the ocean for fish, or fishers of catfish, pretending that these disgusting bottom feeders were some kind of accomplishment! Even I knew not to keep a catfish or even get one on the line. Even worse, Mr. Kang and Abeoji began giving gifts to their customers upon departure. They presented drunken businessmen and weekend warriors with fishing vests and their own individualized lures, even bringing out half-sized foldout chairs to sit on the deck of the boat, watching dayglo bobbers float on top of the water, Abeoji tossing out cups of dayglo chum, spending more time taking pictures of each other than fishing. Mr. Kang and Abeoji even stooped to befriending the customers. They would toast cups of soju and say, "You are my brother," to men that had only met that morning! Mr. Kang, of course, nearly leaping off the boat in the afternoon to fish on his own to keep the restaurants happy, but even the after-hours fish seemed to sense something was up, and the two could not find a drunker drunk to fill the void. Fakes. Both of them. Until Seong reappeared, looking more like a lost brother of Seong than Seong, black slacks and a silken floral shirt, shiny black leather loafers two inches longer than his normal shoes. Not a splotch of paint anywhere.

"You're back!" I shouted to Seong.

"Nope," he said to me. "I'm never coming back. My days on the water are finished."

"Let me guess," Mr. Kang said to Seong. "You sold a painting."

"Sold a painting?" Seong asked.

"A taste of success," Abeoji said. "Congratulations."

Seong bowed slightly to each of them individually. "I did not sell a painting," he said.

My heart sank. How had all three of them converted into abject failures overnight? Looking at Seong was like looking at Abeoji and Mr. Kang. Once great at what they do, now decked out in fancy clothes, but still lonely men, worn out, condemned to solitude and manual labor.

"I sold all of the paintings," Seong said.

"My God," Abeoji said.

"You sold all of the paintings," Mr. Kang said.

"That's right," he said. "A gallery owner from New York City walked into the gallery, spent the day, half of the time on an international call back home."

"How do you know all he wants is sex?" Mr. Kang said to Seong, winking at Abeoji.

"It's a she," Seong said, "who bought the paintings. And if all she wants is sex, that's okay, too."

"Good point," Abeoji said.

"So," Mr. Kang said. "You are going to Seoul."

"No," Seong said. "I hate Seoul. I'm moving to Philadelphia."

"Why not New York?" Mr. Kang said.

"One day. For now, it's too expensive. The gallery owner has an apartment in Philadelphia. It's cheap. I can stay there and paint. She'll come down and buy the paintings she wants. It's a perfect set up."

"And no sex," Mr. Kang said.

"I hope so."

Mr. Kang sat down. Electricity sang between all four of us.

"How many paintings?" Abeoji said.

"Twenty-three."

"In one day," Mr. Kang said.

"In one day."

Seong explained that his small paintings had gone for four hundred thousand won each, and there were only five small paintings. His standard size ranged from sixty by ninety centimeters, which pulled in over five million won each, and then he had a monster two by three-meter canvas that he had to roll up and re-stretch. And because the gallery had been rented, the gallery in Seoul claimed no right to any commission.

"Since we paid the fee," Mr. Kang said.

"That's right," Seong said, beaming.

"Well played," Mr. Kang said.

Abeoji looked at me, then Seong.

Myself, I tried doing the math, but I kept losing track. Was he a millionaire? Was he rich? Seong said he was going to talk to Omoni later that afternoon. She could tell him what to do about taxes, how to handle the money so he doesn't go broke by next week.

"That's right," Abeoji said. "Don't gamble it all away."

"Don't worry, old men," Seong said. "I didn't forget about you." He pulled out of his back pocket a piece of paper, which he unfolded and handed to Abeoji. He stepped into the boat, and Abeoji and Seong pressed their thumbs into red ink and then onto the paper. "The island is yours." And then the closest I had ever seen Abeoji and Mr. Kang coming to blows—Abeoji wrestled Mr. Kang's arm free, but by the time Abeoji had forced Mr. Kang's thumb into the ink as well, Seong's motorbike had already sang into the streets of Jisepo.

"*The island is yours.*" That sentence rang in my head. Seong. What a scam artist. That island. That islet, the seamount, weathered and beaten down by salt, sea and time. Giving Abeoji and Mr. Kang that island was like having a cancerous tumor removed from your back and handing it to your friend. "Here you go—thank you for making me rich!"

XIV

I know why my father had stamped Mr. Kang as his partner in the ownership of Seong's island. If my father had left him out, how would he have gotten to the island? His eyes were not good enough to drive on his own, and he loathed taking the bus. He could have taken the fishing boat, which would have chugged enough gasoline to nullify any profits once he did strike it rich with pearls. Or, he would have to buy his own small boat and hitch it all the way down to Nambu, then find a place to dock the boat and risk having the boat getting all dinged up on the granite walls of the island. Besides, was he going to do this alone, or worse, trust me to be his only partner? Heaven forbid.

My mother would have been happier if Abeoji had invited Mr. Kang to live with us. When Abeoji showed her the papers, she tightened her lip, walked into the bedroom and began packing her bags.

"Where's she going?" I asked Abeoji.

"Boston," she said. "I'm going to live with your sister."

"She's in medical school," Abeoji said.

"She'll need somebody to clean for her," she said.

"She's doing fine," he said.

"She can't cook for herself either."

"You're not going anywhere," Abeoji said.

"I can go anywhere," Omoni said.

"Then go."

"You and Mr. Kang are fishermen!" she said. "You catch fish. You sell fish. Just *fish*. All you want is to create more paperwork for me!"

Abeoji left the room and opened a bottle of Munhak soju. "Here," he said to me, pouring a cup. The idea of another fistful of nails scraping my esophagus terrified me, but I drank it down, and the burning was less than expected. Immediately a warm wave of relief passed through my mind. Not so bad.

"You think she'll really leave?" I asked Abeoji.

"No," Abeoji said. "She loves money. More paperwork means more money."

But I could hear her screaming in the bedroom. She emerged into the living room with the cane. "You knew about this," she said to me, but before I could answer, I scooted back crablike blocking her blows with the bamboo. But I knew she was staying as well. The blows did not feel great, but she was holding back—she knew she had to at least complete the act. She returned to the bedroom to fetch her bags and set them by the front door.

"You are going to own an island with a communist," she said to Abeoji.

"An anarchist," he corrected her.

"Which flag are you going to wave over the island, huh?"

"No flag," Abeoji said. "Flags are stupid."

"He's a traitor."

"He's a friend. Kang Jin is a trusted partner, and he knows the water."

"He's probably Chinese. Have you seen his passport?"

"He is not Chinese."

"I bet he is an infiltrator."

"He's just as Korean as you and me," Abeoji said.

"Not he isn't. He is thankless. He is ungrateful for the sacrifices that we have made for this country."

"No, he isn't. He just hates every leader. Face it. He has a point. They're all a bunch of animals."

Omoni tried to hit Abeoji with the bamboo stick, but he caught his end with his bare hand.

"Hajima," he said.

"This is bad luck. I went to a fortune teller, and she said there was bad news on the horizon."

"There's *always* bad news on the horizon!"

"This is different," she said.

Abeoji had told me numerous times on the water that any number of things could go wrong at any moment. You should always behave on the boat as if disaster was about to strike. You could see a storm on the horizon and fail to estimate the speed and trajectory of the clouds. You could run into a sandbar and destroy your motor, miles from help. Rogue waves. You could have a gas leak. You could flood the engine. You could slip and bang your head. You could fall out of the boat. You could get stiffed by your client. You could get too drunk or dehydrated. You could run out of beer. I wanted to add, as he recounted these possible nightmare scenarios to Omoni, that you could also drive the boat straight into a monolith of tetrapods, but I held back. "Your job as a captain," Abeoji told Omoni, "is to foresee all of these possible calamities and steer around them. That's your job. That is my only job. In other words, my job is a fortune teller! Bad luck is going out there blind or alone. And worse luck is not taking a man like Kang Jin who can single handedly avoid half of these situations without even trying."

Omoni picked up her bags. "I can't believe you're a communist."

"Oh, my God," Abeoji said.

Omoni picked up her bags, slipped into her shoes, and walked out. Abeoji and I walked to the window and could see her carrying her bags down the concrete paths toward Highway 14. We watched her walk all the way down to the bus stop next to the Seven Eleven.

"She's gone," I said to Abeoji.

"There isn't another bus for two hours," Abeoji said. "Besides, she doesn't know there are pearls on the island."

"Are there really pearls?" I said.

"Who knows? Maybe." Abeoji walked across the room and sat at the table. He poured a glass for himself and then nodded his head at me, suggesting that I go busy myself elsewhere. "And don't drink anymore of my goddamned soju."

XV

The next morning, on Monday, the first of Abeoji and Mr. Kang's standard two days off, I walked downstairs. Downstairs, Omoni served up a breakfast of pumpkin pancakes with a bowl of bean paste soup. She gave me a bowl of milk and asked me if I didn't want a bottle of yogurt.

"You're still here," I said.

"Of course," she said. "Here," she set out a plate of peppers cooked with garlic.

"I thought you were going to Boston?"

"How can I go to Boston?"

"I don't know."

"Exactly. You don't know. Who would cook for you?"

"I can cook for myself."

"You can't cook."

"I can."

"Who would do the books around here? The business would go to pieces."

"We could hire somebody to do the books."

"Hire someone you never met to do the books? You think that's a good idea?"

"Sure."

"You don't think they would steal half the money?"

"Hire someone you trust," I said.

"You don't think I can do them? Why would I hire someone I trust if I can do the books?"

"If you were going to Boston."

"If they do the books well enough, they won't be trustworthy."

"Why not?"

"Why do you think?"

"I thought you were moving out," I said.

"It sounds like you want me to leave," she said. "Your father is a dreamer," she said, "but if they do discover any pearls on that island, he won't have any idea what to do with them. He'll probably use them as bait."

Abeoji skipped breakfast that morning, but we left the house and walked the concrete paths along the garden farms and grandmothers, down to the 67-1 bus stop with five rolls of kimbap, two one point five plastic bottles filled with makgeolli, a plastic container filled rice balls stuffed with kimchi, a dozen boiled eggs, a bottle of soy sauce, seven sleeves of oranges, peaches and a tube of tooth glue.

Omoni looked at the provisions and asked when we would be back.

"Tonight," Abeoji said.

"Don't let Kang ajushee bring his communist friends."

"Don't worry."

"I do worry."

"I know."

"Here," she said and gave my father a fifty thousand won note. "Put it in your wallet."

"I have money."

"Doesn't matter. Keep it in your wallet. Just in case."

"There's no place to spend the money."

"It's good luck."

"We have brains to rely on," Abeoji said, pointing to his head.

Omoni kept her hand extended, Abeoji took the money and stuffed it in his wallet.

Abeoji and I arrived at the docks where Mr. Kang was already preparing his dingy for the journey south.

Along with our own food, Mr. Kang was loading the boat down with a box of Hite beer, cases of cheongju, a box full of Munhak. You would have thought we would be gone for weeks, not twelve hours. At the front of the boat, they had another twelve plastic bottles of water, though Abeoji said that Seong claimed there was a well on the island, and once we got it primed and pumping, we would have all the fresh water we needed. "Why don't we just start building on the island?" Mr. Kang said. "We could turn it into a resort!"

For two leathered old fishermen, their eyes ten times bigger than their stomachs, I had never seen them happier.

It didn't take too long before the two began arguing over what they would name the island. "What do you suggest?" they said, when they saw me.

"Island Seong," I said without hesitation.

"Shut up kid, you'll scare the fish," Mr. Kang said, to Abeoji's delight.

"What about 'The Rock of Yi Soon-shin?'" Abeoji said.

"That's sacrilegious," Mr. Kang said. "How about Pearl Island?"

"That sounds like a brothel," Abeoji said.

"It's supposed to," Mr. Kang said, and they both laughed.

"Don't be so goddamned obvious," Abeoji said.

The two of them mused and made fun of each other, belittled me and came up with one idiot name after another, before finally, Mr. Kang said, "The People's Island."

My God. I could see the gleam in my father's eye, when, in the future, at some date, near or far, but inevitably, should they strike it rich with pearls and allow my mother the paperwork she lusted after so passionately, the dark cloud that would erupt into torrents when my mother would learn of the name: *The People's Island.* She would break ceramic bowls, heave her fists at Abeoji, probably thrash me with the bamboo stick, but as always, the view of the numbers would come floating down into her view and peace would again fall upon the household.

A neighbor's car pulled up, and Omoni ran out of the car towards us at the docks. "Don't go!" she yelled.

"What are you talking about?" my father shouted back, while I still held the rope connecting us to the dock.

"I can't take this anymore," Mr. Kang said. "She's worse than the police."

"After the two of you left, a crow landed on the door to the gate outside. I threw rocks at it, but it wouldn't move."

"So what?"

"You are all going to die!"

"Stop," Abeoji said. "What did I tell you?"

"This is too obvious," Mr. Kang said.

"I beg you," she said. "Kang son-sang-nim can even come to the house if you don't go on this trip."

"Forget it," Abeoji said. "We're going."

"Then leave the boy. He stays."

Abeoji grabbed the rope and pulled us to the dock. "Take him."

"Go on," Mr. Kang said, and I stepped off the boat onto the dock.

As Mr. Kang's dingy drifted from the dock, he shot back at Omoni, "Maybe it's you who are going to die!"

Oh, my God, my bowels dropped and sank into hot soup. Did he really say that to Omoni?

She picked up a stone and heaved the rock with far greater accuracy than I would have imagined, banging the rock off the aluminum hull. She fired off another stone that bounced off the lip of the dingy and ricocheted between the two men.

Mr. Kang waved by to Omoni, and she fired another stone landing wildly short. Mr. Kang cranked the engine, and they were off.

XVI

Omoni and I rode the 67-1 home in silence. Of course, Omoni was not silent because she was mad at Abeoji or Mr. Kang, she had incredible recovery time with her anger. She could chase me around the house beating brutally with the bamboo cane, then hear the phone ringing and launch into the most pleasant conversation with her lady friends, still holding the bamboo cane. However, it occurred to me that the two of us had sat and walked home in silence because she had utterly no idea of what to say to me. What were my interests in life? Did I, by any chance, enjoy spending day after day on the boat with Abeoji and Mr. Kang? Was I learning anything that might help me on the middle school exams? Had I signed up for the exams? I took a chance, myself. I mustered up the courage, learned forward to the seat in front of me and tapped Omoni on the arm.

"Huh?" she said.

"Omoni. Do you think Abeoji and Mr. Kang will even find any pearls?"

Omoni placed a finger to her lips then pointed to a sign on the bus instructing passengers to refrain from talking. We were the only two on the bus.

We walked home in silence as well. I took off before she could rope me into practicing languages or doing some random math homework. I bolted out the door and took the back paths toward the Mangchi pier. On the way, I broke a small bamboo tree at the joint, snapping the stalk clean. I bought a roll of monofilament and a box of hooks from the fishing store next to the mart and decided to try my luck fishing with all of the weekend anglers and posers. I have to admit, as much as Mr. Kang belittled me and irritated me, nevermind the politics, I thought about what he might do in a situation like this. The truth is, the row of fishermen and women on each side of the pier depressed me. They sat in their chairs, half of them carrying on conversations in full volume, hackling and laughing it up as if the fish could not pick up on the vibrations. Didn't they even want to catch fish? One fisherman even used a camera fixed to a drone above the water, whizzing away. Unbelievable! The idea of it all. To toil and slave away at some mind-numbing job in the city, a boss booming down on you, wives and children picking your spirit clean, only to spend your one day off in the week pretending to do something that you had no aptitude at all. I pitied them.

Suddenly, I felt like a pro compared to these people. Since I had no bait for starters, I tried to catch water bugs darting along the surface of the pier. The little demons moved so quickly, and just as you were about to pick them up, even if you got your fingers on one, all of their scales and feet spooked you. What if they crawled up your arm, down your shirt? What if they crawled in your ear? What then? Would they begin feeding, laying eggs? Who knows? Finally, I had one under my palm, and turns out, they're harmless. I sank the hook through their soft tissue between the chinks in their armor. Ready to go. I tossed the line out and waited.

Eventually, of course, sitting on the warm concrete pier, listening to the ebb and flow of the waves, the cool breeze and humidity of the salty air, I fell asleep. I don't know why but I dreamed that I had fallen asleep on the surface of the moon, and during the day, the bright side of the moon heats up so much you can boil water, and I had forgotten all about this, but in my state, I could not move a muscle. Paralyzed, I could feel my insides cooking. My flesh smelled horrific, like bubbling sulfur, fat oozing and organs tenderizing as my belly turned into a living stew. The stench grew so foul that the smell attracted pigs that came down from the mountainsides to feed from my belly, digging deep with their snouts and tangling my intestines on their tusks, creating the most terrible sounds, ggool-ggool, bubbling up through the fluids, ggool-ggool, muffled by flesh and ribcage, the pigs pulling out my insides, stringing along my guts, running with them, until suddenly, I woke up in the dream and realized that this meant a fish must be running with my bait. Shocked to my senses, the sun blasting a nuclear flash to my retinas, the sound of the bamboo absorbing straight into the water, leaving behind a trail of bubbles. A *third* fishing pole lost to the sea. To my horror, I looked up, shielding the sun with my hands, and wouldn't you know it? A group of college students stood next to me, the sun blocked by their bodies. They had watched the entire process and could not stop hooting and laughing. How cute!

He's adorable! What a show! Each of them held in front of them a camera, filming the whole thing. They even filmed me running along the side of the beach parking lot toward Highway 14, where I picked up a stone and tossed it in their direction, only adding humiliation upon humiliation as their laughter increased.

When I returned home, however, I remembered the pigs. So many of them. My stomach even hurt remembering the dream. I told my mother about the dream, and she leapt from the floor and threw her arms around me. "Do you know what this means?" she said. "The pigs?"

"No," I said.

"They've found the pearls! Where there is one, there are many. Abeoji and Kang Jin have found the pearls. We're rich!"

That night I fell asleep with the window open, hoping to be awakened when my father returned, ready for a celebration. I could hear Omoni downstairs talking to her sisters and friends, exchanging pleasantries, talking about her husband, the fisherman and adventurer, how, in the end, he always makes the right decision, his wisdom. She talked about pigs and pearls, and there would be enough for everybody. There would be so many pearls they wouldn't know what to do with them. I could see the pearls themselves, forming in the darkness in my vision. Eventually, I acquiesced to sleep—maybe I would dream of even more pigs.

XVII

Tuesday morning, I awoke, and my father was already sitting in the living room eating a bowl of fish soup and rice for breakfast. Wedges of a white peach sat on a plate in the middle of the table. His eyes seemed to have sunk deep in his head, as if he had just returned from a lengthy and serious hospital stay, the whites of his eyes completely transformed into red. He forked a wedge of peach and shoved it in his mouth, swallowing in one motion.

"Did we find any pearls yesterday?" I asked Abeoji.

"No pearls yesterday."

"Even any oysters?"

"Not that I know of."

"But I dreamed of a pig yesterday."

"You were probably hungry."

"You should look for pearls closer to home," Omoni said.

Abeoji still stank of alcohol. My guess was that he and Mr. Kang had not even slept, and here they were about to go out for the second day in a row, three weeks into spending their days off on the island.

"You shouldn't even go looking for pearls at all," Omoni said. "The fishing charter is doing fine. After all, we're business owners, and our daughter is going to be a doctor."

"Why did you guys decide to help out Seong, anyway?" I asked.

Abeoji gave me a look and motioned with his eyeballs that Omoni was still in the room and to keep quiet if I knew what was good for me. I had forgotten about all of the extra money he and Mr. Kang had failed to report.

Omoni sat down next to me and said, "Your father has decided that he is going to work through the night on every one of his days off from now on, so he can bring back no pearls and die early of exhaustion, unless he drowns of exhaustion before then. Isn't that nice? When he is home, he will be unrested and short-tempered. But don't worry, soon we will have a picture on the wall, a very nice picture of your own father, maybe even painted by Comrade Kang, himself, hanging above an urn of his ashes."

"*Aye-shh*," Abeoji said. Abeoji said he was going to be buried in a tomb, like everybody else.

"Those days are gone," Omoni said. "Nobody's using tombs anymore. You think the younger generation is going to take care of the grass and weeds? Come to see us on the Day of the Dead and feed us snacks and soju?"

"Yes," he said.

"Fat chance," she said. "You're willing to risk that kind of bad luck by having an unkempt grave?"

"Yes," he said.

"You think *he* is going to take care of your grave?" she said, nodding at me.

Abeoji looked at me then forked another wedge of peach.

"Well, you won't be around to make those decisions, working like you do," Omoni said. "You'll be gone in a matter of months living like this. At your age! You should at least wait until your daughter finishes medical school. I should start taking suitors and preparing for my life for when that day comes."

"Maybe you should," Abeoji said.

"I won't be grieving for three years if you keep this up."

"I'll be dead if I *don't* go looking for pearls," he said.

Omoni left the room and turned on the television. She sank herself into her favorite new television program, a show on at any station at any time, of some poor, overworked youngster, singing and dancing, only to have a panel of judges, composed of washed-up pop stars, hem and haw, critiquing their skills of imitation and idiocy.

"Why did Omoni say Mr. Kang would paint your portrait?" I said to Abeoji.

"He's not going to."

"He paints?" I said.

"Aye-shh!"

"Why did she say that?"

"He *was* a painter, when he was younger."

"When he was Seong's age?"

"Something like that."

"Really?"

"Can I eat peacefully?" Abeoji said. "Yes, really."

"Ah," I said. "I remember he painted the picture on the restaurant sign."

"That was years ago, and never speak of this," Abeoji said. "Especially to Mr. Kang."

"Why not?"

"Just don't."

"Does he wish he could paint now?"

"Probably not. Men live to work, not to dream. The faster your dreams die, the happier you will be."

"What about Jin-soo? What about her dream of being a doctor?"

"Her dream isn't to be a doctor. It's your mother's dream for her to be a doctor. Jin-soo is just obliging your mother, as she should."

"You didn't dream of being a fisherman?"

"Of course not."

"What did you want to be?"

"I don't remember."

"But you love fishing."

"I love that I am good at fishing. But I could care less. I am a good fisherman because it is my job."

"I bet Mr. Kang wasn't a very good painter."

Abeoji sat up straight. I could tell from the look on his face that if I were a stranger, and if we were out drinking, or even outside of the house, then these words might function as an invitation to fight, and my own back straightened in a reflex of self-defense.

"Mr. Kang was an excellent painter," Abeoji said. "Mr. Kang is a master."

"Really?"

"Of course! Did you think he would not be good?"

"Maybe."

"Is he a good fisherman?"

"Yes."

"People who are good at one thing, are often good at many things."

"What did he paint?"

Abeoji lifted his bowl and finished off the broth from his fish soup. "Mr. Kang painted portraits of Park Chung-hee. Life-sized portraits. Sometimes, Mr. Kang painted portraits only of Park's face. Sometimes, he painted large images of Park's kettle of makgeolli." Abeoji spoke with his hands, creating imaginary images of the kettle of makgeolli and the shape of Park Chung-hee's face. "The attention to detail was like real life, photographic, but with its own sense of life."

"I thought Mr. Kang hated Park Chung-hee."

"He does!"

"My God," I said.

"That's right," he said.

"What happened?"

"Simple," Abeoji said. "Mr. Kang gained some attention, due to his craft. He had many followers."

"So?"

"So—he held an exhibition in Seocho. Turns out, there was a misunderstanding. Many people said that Mr. Kang was a fine painter, and as these discussions go, a policeman suggested that Mr. Kang was not a fine painter, but Mr. Kang was only fortunate to have such a fine subject. One thing turned into another, and the policeman suggested that, after all, who knows whether or not the images were painted out of sarcasm or sincere affection? As Mr. Kang does not back down from these sorts of accusations, it wasn't too long before a busload of policemen showed up and ripped the paintings down from the wall. They ripped the paintings apart and even set some to flame in the street. Now, another group of supporters got the idea that Mr. Kang was burning images of Park Chung-hee himself. Next on the list for the policemen was Kang Jin himself."

"Did they catch him?"

"Do you think they did?"

"No."

"That's right. Mr. Kang ran through the neighborhoods of Seoul and hopped on a train southward, and that was it. He lived for months as a vagrant in Busan, but vagrants had a difficult time during those days, and eventually he walked to Geoje-do and lived on the beaches and rocks. He spent years in Tonyeong and Namhae, too. That was when he taught himself how to fish and find all of the best spots. See, if you are sleeping in the park, on a doorstep, or in the woods, then you are a vagrant, and you could be sent to forced labor. But if you are sleeping on the beach with a line in the water, then you're not a vagrant at all. You are a fisherman. Soon, he began selling extra fish to ajumas with soju tents, but eventually, he saved enough for more equipment, and soon enough, he had enough for a small boat. Next thing you know, he was selling fish to restaurants."

"He still sells fish to restaurants."

"Exactly."

"The police didn't keep looking for him?"

"They did for a while, but they had larger targets. Believe me, they had their hands full in those days."

"What about now?"

"Now, they could care less. But he's got his own system now. He has, for years. When Seong worked for us, and we discovered that Seong was a painter, Mr. Kang couldn't wait for the chance to send him up to Seoul. Seong has no idea about this, but this was Seong's only chance for success. Mr. Kang would have put every penny of his earnings into Seong's future."

XVIII

After five weeks of working five days straight, sunrise to sunset, only to spend two of Abeoji's days off on The People's Island, usually without sleep, returning dirty, stinking of fish and booze and mud, Omoni began to become suspicious. "If there are no oysters on the island," she said, "then there are no pearls. I think you can call off the expedition."

"The oysters are there," Abeoji said, "we just have to find them. If we can't find them, then we'll transplant the oysters."

"Oh, that sounds like a simple operation," she said.

"This is Mr. Kang's handiwork," Omoni said.

"Leave Mr. Kang out of it. Enough with Mr. Kang."

"Are you sure that both of you are looking for pearls the whole time on the island?"

"Working to the bone," Abeoji said.

"Then why do you smell like alcohol? Can you drink

soju underwater?"

"At the end of the day, we celebrate a solid effort."

"What time does the end of the day begin?"

"Same as everybody else."

"I didn't see any snorkeling equipment on the boat when I dropped you off a few weeks ago."

"We free dive."

"Who free dives?"

"I do, and Kang Jin. We free dive."

"How far can you free dive?"

"As far as I need to."

"I don't believe you. I don't trust you, and I certainly do not trust Kang Jin."

"What's new?"

"Next week, you're taking him with you," Omoni said, pointing at me.

"No, Omoni," I said.

"If you're there, they won't get into trouble," she said to me.

"Yes, they will," I protested.

"Well, what are you doing here?" she asked me. "Are you doing your math homework?"

"Yes," I said.

"Show me. Show me one math problem you've done over the past month."

"I will. I'll start. I promise."

"This is why your sister is going to be a doctor. She did her math homework. And nobody had to tell her to do her homework."

"Because she's a goody-goody."

"Have you been playing piano?"

"I don't like piano."

"Are you reading?"

"I hate reading."

"Then you'll work."

"It's too dangerous for him," Abeoji said. "There are cliffs on the island. The ground is too unstable."

"The men are too unstable!" Omoni said.

"There are poisonous snakes."

"How do snakes get on the island?" she asked.

"How do I know?" Abeoji said. "I don't question these things."

"I don't want to go," I said.

"He doesn't want to go," Abeoji said. "Let him be a kid for once. Let him make mud pies and play with bugs."

"I'm not a child," I said.

"Life will be miserable soon enough for him. He'll go to high school, and they will ruin him. And then he will go to college and get trained to be a stooge in some office. Then he'll go to the military service, get V.D. from a whore, get married and live where he never wanted to live. He's got two, maybe three years of possible happiness left, and he's probably not happy now. Are you happy?" he asked me.

"No," I said.

"Then he can be unhappy with you," she said. "He has no idea how hard life is."

"No," Abeoji said. "He needs to have free time."

"When did you make up your mind about this?" she said. "You hate free time! What's gotten into you?"

"Now," Abeoji said. "I just decided. I had a revelation."

"Okay," Omoni said. "Fine. It's too dangerous for a young boy to go."

"Right," Abeoji said. "See?"

"I'll go," she said. "You both could use some good cooking, and I'm sure the camp you set up is filthy. You need a woman's presence to keep you in line."

"Come, then," Abeoji said. "You can help me and Mr.

Kang sweep the snakes from under the mat and latrine. God knows it is miserable shoo-ing those creatures away when you try and do your business."

Omoni squared her jaw and looked at Abeoji. Oh, there were a handful of maneuvers at play in her mind. You can be straight up divorced, that was a single consideration, along with sabotaging Kang Jin's dingy in the middle of the night—sending the two on a suicide mission and spending the next year or so doing her best grieving impression to satisfy neighbors and relatives. To be sure, she considered calling the old man's bluff and going along, but the thought of snakes—Abeoji, and I knew as well—was too much for her to bear— especially the thought of snakes crawling beneath her while she used the bathroom. Or she could force me to go. In the end, she chose the latter. If one of us had to get bitten by a poisonous viper, fifty kilometers from the nearest hospital, and probably only accessible by helicopter, it might as well be me. By the end of breakfast, she had packed my bags herself.

XX

Abeoji and I walked along the Gujora docks to meet Mr. Kang. Heat radiated so intensely from the morning sun my scalp burned beneath my hair, and my hair itself felt hot to the touch. Water splashing onto the concrete docks evaporated in seconds. I tried putting on a straw hat, which provided a moment of relief from the sun's radiation, but the hat heated up and burned my scalp anyway. "It's too hot," I said to Abeoji.

"Then drink water," he said.

The two of us walked along the pier and the line of fishing boats. None of the regular morning ajushee were there, taking their day off like normal people, sleeping off their hangovers and allowing their muscles to rest and return to form. We could only see Mr. Kang down the line, loading cases and boxes. Even from that distance, Mr. Kang looked exhausted and overheated. As we approached, Mr. Kang slowed, placed one hand on his hip and pointed our direction. "What the hell is the kid coming with us for?"

"No other choice," Abeoji said. "It was him or my wife."

"Like hell there was no other choice," he said. "You could have murdered him on the walk here."

"Believe me," Abeoji said, "I thought about it."

Together, the three of us loaded up the food and pushed away from the dock. Mr. Kang hoisted a bottle of Munhak and took in half the bottle in one pull.

"It wasn't his fault," Abeoji said.

"Of course, it was his fault," Mr. Kang said.

"We're coming home without any pearls. What is my wife supposed to think? Of course, she's going to be suspicious."

"Suspicious of what?" I asked.

"Shut up kid. You'll scare the fish," Mr. Kang said.

"Nothing," Abeoji said. "Suspicious that we are not cut out to be pearl divers. Is that such a crime?"

"I guess not," I said.

"Damn right," Abeoji said.

"Yeah," Mr. Kang said. "But your boy is lazy. Your wife could care less about us. She wants us out of the house. She's mad because he's not getting anything done in the day, and she's taking it out on you. You doing your homework?" Mr. Kang asked me.

"No," I said.

"You fold your blankets this morning?"

"I didn't have a chance. Omoni did it before I could finish breakfast."

"You have to beat her to it. You have to fold your blankets before you eat breakfast," Mr. Kang said. "You play piano every day?"

"No," I said.

"See?" Mr. Kang said, then turned his attention to Abeoji. "You are pulling your weight. Your wife is making a fortune off of you and our charter business."

"She is?" I said.

"No," Abeoji said.

"Like hell, she isn't. We make a lot of money with our business. She puts all the money away. Credit to her for that. You spend all your extra money. You don't build a fortune. But that doesn't matter when your kid is as lazy as he is."

"My daughter isn't lazy," Abeoji said. "She's going to be a doctor."

"I'm not lazy," I said.

"*Aye-shh!*" Mr. Kang said.

"Shut up, Mr. Kang," I said. "You'll scare away the people."

"Son of a bitch," Mr. Kang said and leapt towards me with his hands aimed for my neck. Abeoji caught him and turned his energy against him, lifting him and setting him back down next to the motor, then turned back towards me and slapped me across the face.

Before I had the chance to hold back my tears and show both of them that neither the words nor the slap hurt me, Mr. Kang cranked the motor, and the drunken drumrolls roared and shot us out to sea. It was no easy feat, though. Abeoji's hand stung, for sure, but a hand is nothing compared to the depth and power of Omoni's bamboo stick. The salt air, though, amplified the pain of each, adding to it the slapping of my hair against my forehead. So, there we were, the three of us looking toward the south in Mr. Kang's dingy. Off to the grand People's Island.

XXI

The People's Island, indeed, was much bigger than I had remembered, both in circumference and height, though in hindsight, we had never come as close to the island as we now were. A tuft of forest topped an otherwise granite rock jutting out of the East Sea. I could not imagine that any moderate typhoon did not send waves over the surface of the island in its entirety, including the trees. Mr. Kang and my father had fixed Styrofoam tubing, encased with aluminum tape, to the side of the dingy to keep the stone walls of the island from scraping. They had also fixed a rope ladder to the top of the face of a stone wall, where we had to load food and drink to our backs while climbing. Abeoji and Mr. Kang went first, the ladder swinging from side to side, muscles bulging on their backs and thighs—muscles that I had never known existed before seeing individuals perform such unusual exercises.

At the top, a natural trail led to the center of the island, where a clearing opened up and the leaders of this small island (in their minds, this small *country*) had built a platform with a makeshift roof. Next to the platform, soju bottles, makgeolli bottles and beer bottles filled two boxes full, and on the other side of the platform, a sign that had been raised, reading, "The People's Island," including a rendering of the island itself, in almost photographic detail.

"I thought it was an islet," I said.

"What do you know?" Mr. Kang said.

"That's a lot of bottles," I said.

"That's a lot of bottles," Mr. Kang said, mimicking me in a baby voice.

"Have you fixed the well, yet?" I asked.

"The well?" Mr. Kang said.

"Abeoji said there was a well," I said.

"There is no well," Mr. Kang said. "How could there be a well? We're out in the middle of nowhere. Who would put a well here?"

"I don't know," I said. "But Abeoji said there was a well."

"Who are you reporting to?" Mr. Kang said.

"Nobody," I said. "I'm just thirsty."

"Then drink from a bottle of water."

I pulled a bottle from the box and took in the water in heaves, and I could feel the water turning my stomach into a sack of fluid. The way the water sloshed, I could feel my stomach as a sack, the shape and thickness of the stomach lining itself.

"Okay, punk," Mr. Kang said. "Time for you to get to work. First of all, we'll need to build a fire at some point, so why don't you gather some wood. Get plenty of small branches to start at first, then bring the bigger ones."

"Where do I find wood?"

"Aye-shh! In the woods," he said. "Gather *dry* branches. You can find driftwood, too, on the beachhead."

"There's a beachhead? Why did we dock the boat on the rock?"

"Because the easy way isn't always the best way."

"But we could get killed climbing up the rock with all of those boxes."

"Aye-shh," he said, motioning for me to get to work and leave him alone.

Abeoji and Mr. Kang got comfortable in the shade. They put out a plate of tomatoes and oranges, then opened a bottle of Munhak, filling their shot glasses and tossing them down. After I returned with one armful of branches, they had switched to makgeolli, which they had transferred from plastic water bottles back home, to a gold-colored aluminum kettle. Although they had already begun to look sleepy, it had yet to approach lunchtime.

After stacking wood, they told me to finish unloading the boat. Every trip back to camp with sacks of provisions, the two seemed to be drinking something different. Cheongju, beer, rice wine, soju, baek-sae-ju. By the time I was finished, they had dozed off to sleep. I woke up my father. "What do I do now?"

"Run along. Busy yourself."

"With what?"

"Fishing."

"Where do we dive for oysters?"

Mr. Kang awoke, briefly, and the two looked at each other. "Dive next to the boat. You can throw any oysters you find into the boat. Bring them up when you're finished, and we'll eat the ones that don't have any pearls."

I walked back to the rope ladder and climbed the rockface down to the boat, where I realized that I did not have any fins, just a mask and snorkel, which would have to work. I could scout the island for now and then haul in my fortune the next day and weeks to follow. I dove in.

Of course, barnacles covered the rocks in massive sheets, a handful of confused looking fish swimming about. The clarity of the water startled me, as I could see hundreds of meters with stark clarity, but there lacked any fishing game except for these confused-looking fish, the size of your fingers, swimming about as if they had been off course for most of their lives.

For a time, I swam, gazing downward, and after a while, my body and mind each took on the spirit of flying. This was the sensation that birds feel, I understood—nothing risky or out of the ordinary. More precisely, it felt as if I were in a dream, and it began to worry me that I would lull myself to sleep, begin to descend, pass out and sail downwards into the abyss. Stupid thoughts. All of them, stupid. No wonder Mr. Kang treated me like a child.

I swam to the north side of the island where the sea shallowed and turned to sand, eventually so shallow

I could stand with my head and shoulders out of the water. When I did, I pulled my mask off, rubbed my eyes and saw another dingy approaching the island. Dear God. No wonder we had no oysters. *Oyster pirates.* Were these bastards coming to the island to scrape the place clean? I looked about and had no idea where our boat had been tied, my bearings completely gone.

Which way should I swim to find the boat? I had completely forgotten to keep an eye out for landmarks or take stock of direction. How far had I swum? Like a dreamer, sleepwalking through life. Serves me right. I wondered if I had even swum to another island! Again, I made peace with myself. I would swim the way I came, and if I died, then I would die. As long as I swam, I gave myself a chance, and if I did succeed, I would show both of them—Abeoji and that animal, Mr. Kang, that I was no kid, that I had saved them from these oyster thieves, whose morality and code of ethics saw no boundaries or any wrongdoing on the open waters. Pirates. However, our boat did come into view, and I climbed in, then shimmied up the ladder. My breathing had increased, and my bowels tightened. I ran in a dancing motion with my feet on the exposed granite, sharp and hot as a stovetop, running down the trail where my father and Mr. Kang sat in the shade, under their makeshift rooftop. Next to them sat three men, the same men from the approaching dingy, each of them with a shot glass, and each with a stack of money so big they had to use a bottle of Munhak as a paperweight. Somewhere deep in my father's stack of money, for certain, lay the fifty thousand won note my mother had stuffed in his pocket that morning.

XXII

The men were not pirates, at all, nor were they thieves, nor oyster poachers. In fact, they had nothing to do with the water or marine life at all. I spent the rest of the afternoon eating rice balls and drinking Pocari Sweat, napping in a cave I had discovered where there was not a well, but a creek that sounded as if it flowed deep within the recesses of the island itself, or perhaps the ocean water streamed through cracks and crevices and was eating the island away from the inside out. Either way, I knew better than to explore too deeply, for fear that I would become a permanent fixture of The People's Island.

When the sun had begun to cast long shadows and twilight darkened mountains in the distance, I returned to the campsite. All of the men were standing around the fire holding sticks, each with a fish at the end.

"We saved you a fish," Abeoji said.

"Where'd they come from?" I said.

"Mr. Kang," Abeoji said. "An hour ago."

"I didn't see any fish down there," I said, and the men laughed.

I took the snapper that Mr. Kang had caught and bit into the cake of the flesh. The fish had been gutted and scaled, cooled just enough where I could eat it comfortably without fear of dripping or burning myself, and the meat pulled effortlessly from the bones. The fish smelled nothing like fish. I would never admit it, but it was the best fish I had ever tasted. Somehow, the protein seemed to immediately have an effect on my muscles, sore from climbing the granite rock face and swimming around the island. Instantly, I felt rejuvenated and nourished.

"What did you season it with?" I asked.

"Season?" Mr. Kang said.

"Yeah. What kind of spices did you add?"

"Nothing. It's just fish."

"Salt," Abeoji said.

"It tastes seasoned," I said.

"It's fresh," Mr. Kang said.

In moments, I held in my hand a complete and fully constructed fish bone, which I tossed into the fire.

"Not bad, huh?" Mr. Kang said.

"So-so," I said.

"So-so," he said, and the men laughed again.

Abeoji explained on the evening boat ride home that the men I had seen were fellow fishermen from Jisepo. They came out to spend the day and play some poker and Go-Stop.

"I thought you were looking for pearls."

"We have found a pearl," Mr. Kang said. "The People's Island."

"Where else are we going to find any peace?" Abeoji said.

"Home," I said.

"What is work?" Mr. Kang asked me abruptly. "Work is what you do to earn money to provide for your family, survive, and if you are lucky, to find peace of mind. We are working here. We have established a community—these are our friends who will look after us if life becomes too difficult. Is it so wrong to enjoy ourselves, to gamble and get drunk without any hassle?"

"Listen," Abeoji said. "This place makes money, too. We help out the men with a day off to relax, and they help us out with other things."

"What things?"

"Who knows? Money. Bait. Information. Fuel. Whatever. Besides, when we started our business, they gave us plenty of recommendations. They supplied us with so many clients, we would have never established ourselves without them."

"Listen punk," Mr. Kang said. "Maybe one day we'll find a pearl. If we do find these pearls, we'll put the island on the market and triple its value—at least. Then, we'll sell The People's Island and split the money after taxes. I'll spend my share, your father will give his share to your mother, and then we'll die. But until that day happens, we have a place to ourselves."

"Was this even Seong's island to give?" I said, suddenly looking at Abeoji and Mr. Kang as if maybe *they* weren't the pirates *themselves.*

Mr. Kang and Abeoji laughed and looked at each other. "We don't even know. But who cares?"

XXIII

As it happened, I learned to enjoy The People's Island. What wasn't there to like? An endless supply of swimming and looking for oysters. Did I find any? Of course, not! But what would I have done if I had found them? My belief that the pearls were down there had engrained itself into a permanent fixture. Those pearls would make me rich one day, but why discover them now when Mr. Kang and Abeoji would just snatch them up and take all the credit? Until then, I had the smell of the pine trees, rich with reproductive vitality—a smell that would one day return to me in the least suspecting and most obvious moments. One moment of adventure followed the next. I even began fishing with homemade bamboo poles and could bring back a basket, fully cleaned and scaled. I gorged on fish. I cooked fish over the fire, and sometimes I ate slabs of flesh raw, peeling the skin from the fish alive, sliding my knife down the backbone and removing a clean filet. I brought back fish to the campsite and boiled them, sometimes in a stew, and sometimes in plain water, eating flakes of fish meat dipped in soy sauce. Abeoji and Mr. Kang even liked the fish I cooked for them. The trick to catching fish was to climb trees overhanging terrifying drops and scout schools of fish. The skills took no time at all to learn. Moments, really, once I was out on my own and away from Abeoji and Mr. Kang. I did not dare tell them my secret for catching fish. I just played dumb, like they did. "Hey Punk, where'd you catch these fish?" *Don't remember.* "How'd you find them?" *How do I know?*

One morning, up in the trees, I spotted another dingy of the same variety of pirates—pirates who took Abeoji and Mr. Kang's money, not by force, but by strategy and systems of chance. I shimmied down the tree and made my way to the landing dock on the beachhead. These pirates were different. A man sat at the tail of the dingy, manning the motor, and two middle-aged ladies, on the late end of middle-age and younger than Abeoji and Mr. Kang. The two ladies removed their heels and stepped onto the sand and kind of danced on their toes avoiding both the heat and the moisture, followed by a different dance altogether when they hit the jagged texture of the granite. One of the women stood quite tall, taller than Abeoji and Mr. Kang, and the other woman stood a hand-length shorter than Abeoji. Each of the women's bodies filled their jumpsuits, breasts heaving, and hair coifed up in a permanent wave. The smaller woman smiled, and I recognized her immediately—the gold tooth gave her away. One of the ladies from the soju tents.

"Watch out for snakes!" I said as they walked ashore.

The two women screamed. "*Where?*" they said.

"I'm talking about my father and his friend," I said. "The worst kind."

Then women laughed, "Ah!" the taller woman said. "You must be Abeoji's son."

"Yes," I said. "I am no relation to the other man."

"Ha," the shorter woman with the gold tooth said. "You could do worse."

"I bet I couldn't," I said.

Both of the women put on their heels, and then the two walked up to me, their heels wobbling dangerously on the granite surface. They bent towards me like they were going to tell me a secret. My eyes, drawn down the cleavage of the woman with the gold tooth, toward the space between her bra and breast, where the edge of her nipple curved just above the fabric. "You don't have any soju, do you?" she said.

"Come with me," I said and led them up the trail, occasionally stamping a bamboo stick on the ground to scare away the snakes and using the stick to also keep passing branches from bending back and slapping them. I turned around and the dingy they had arrived in had already departed, now, hundreds of meters from The People's Island. The whine of the dingy sounding like a buzz saw carving the water in half. We continued walking, and the taller woman grabbed my hand for assistance and then would not let go. I was not sure exactly why she would not let go, but I liked the feeling of it and did not protest as we made our way to the platform and makeshift roof.

Abeoji and Mr. Kang were absent upon our arrival, but I opened a bottle of makgeolli for the two and poured them each a paper cup of the rice wine. The women drank down their makgeolli, and I refilled their cups. I gave them the entire bottle, and the two retreated to the platform. The taller woman told me to come hither, and she placed the bottle to my lips, leaned my head backwards, then suddenly squeezed the bottle. The wine thrusted out, forcing into me half the bottle in one pull. My first taste of makgeolli ever. It was as if my body had vomited in reverse.

I left the two women there and told them that my father and Mr. Kang would be back soon. Evidently, I needed to get a good jump on fishing. It would be dinnertime soon. I didn't know we were expecting company.

XXIV

Mr. Kang was right. When you knew where the fish were, what they were eating, when they liked to eat, and how what they liked to eat behaved, at what temperature, fishing was a breeze. You needed none of the extra materials and equipment. You didn't need a special chair that held bottles or cups, or a special jacket with special pockets and clips, nor did you need special shoes, or special rigs, or special lights on the end of the rod, or on the bobber, or be on the pier or in the water. You just needed the critical information. With each fish I caught for our guests, I looped a string through their gills and out their mouths, tied the string to a tree and tossed them back in the water to keep them fresh. In no time, I had five fish, which were still alive when I scaled them, their muscles suddenly contracting, bending their body into the physical representation of fear. The eyes of the fish, if they could have widened, they would have, and if they could have opened wider, they would have spoken. I slit the fish from the bottom of their jaw, down the belly to the tail and scraped their insides, the jewels and tubes spilling into the water. I took some salt from my pockets and rubbed the fish inside and out, let the juices get flowing before roasting them above the fire.

When I returned, Mr. Kang was sitting next to the shorter woman on the platform.

"Where's Abeoji?" I said.

"Hm…" Mr. Kang said. "Where is he?" He turned his attention to the woman. "Do you know where he went?"

"No."

"Me neither," Mr. Kang said. "I think he's working on the well. I think he is trying to get some fresh water."

"I thought there was no well."

"*Aye-shhh*," Mr. Kang said.

"Where is the other woman?" I said.

"She's freshening up," the shorter woman with the gold tooth said.

"How can she freshen up without a well? We've got no fresh water."

"He's an interrogator," Mr. Kang said to the woman.

"He's a good one," she said.

"He should be a cop," Mr. Kang said.

"He's too cute to be a cop."

"You've been drinking too much," Mr. Kang said to her.

"Why don't you start cooking the fish?" the woman said to me. "I hear you're a good cook."

"From who?" I said.

"That's right," Mr. Kang said. "The little bastard is such a good cook, I'm beginning to rethink my opinion of him."

Flattered, somewhat, I fixed the fish on bamboo and held a fish in each hand over the fire, turning them on one side, then turning them on the other, letting the juices drip and sing on the coals. I cooked all five and lined them up on a plate, each of the faces on the fish frozen in expressions of horror.

The woman left and returned shortly with the taller woman, and then the shorter woman and Mr. Kang left together without eating.

"Where's Abeoji?" I asked the woman.

"Oh, my God," the woman said. "Give me a fish. I feel like I haven't eaten in weeks."

I handed the woman a stick, and together, we ate rockfish. The woman groaned as she ate, smacking her teeth and sucking each bone clean, then flicking the bone into the darkness, her fingers working the meat with delicate dexterity. The woman placed chopsticks of rice in her mouth between each bite of fish. She placed the head of the fish to her lips and sucked out one eyeball, then turned the fish over and sucked out the other, and then bit the top portion of the head clean off, crunching the bones into gravel, her own face a perfect combination of pleasure and pain, until she worked the food down and took another bite.

I poured the woman a paper cup filled halfway with Munhak, and she washed it down in one shot. I filled her cup a second and third time.

"Don't you want a drink?" she said.

"Okay," I said, and she filled a cup for me as well.

"You're a good drinker," she said.

I thanked her and we took turns filling the cup until the bottle was empty.

"Do you want another fish?" I asked her.

"God, no," she said, rubbing her belly.

"Rice?"

"Why don't you go down to the beach and see if you can find your father."

Feeling drunk, I walked in the moonlight as if the vision was in fact the sight of another person, channeling the vision into my own brain. The ocean, new ocean, the trees, new trees, and the sky shining cold light on the water surrounding. I walked to the beachhead and over by the caves, listening to the water trickle deep in the sternum of the island, and I took the trail to the granite rock face where the ladder descended to the dingy. Abeoji was nowhere to be found, but the moonlight shining on the water below was something to behold, and the island itself seemed to rock gently in the waves.

XXV

It became clear to me that we were not going home for the evening when I returned to see the four of them sitting around the campfire, the glow of fire dancing on each of their faces. They were now eating freshly cooked corn, the women picking kernel by kernel, seemingly to avoid appearing barbaric and tearing into the corn like animals. To be honest, I noticed something about how Mr. Kang ate his corn, picking also kernel by kernel, but thoughtfully, as if to weigh the bulk of his life experiences and determining the balance of his integrity from a position where all hope was probably lost.

They held out cups for each other and drank. I could not understand exactly what they were discussing, but every moment or so, each of them would laugh heartily, which I found difficult to believe, since, at least in the case of Abeoji and Mr. Kang, each lacked any sense of humor whatsoever. Not a drop between the two of them combined.

I stood, found my footing as I stepped off the platform and approached the four. "What are you laughing at?" I asked them.

"Nothing," Abeoji said. "We will keep it down. Go to sleep. It's late."

"Tell him," Mr. Kang said.

"Tell him nothing," Abeoji said again. "It's not important."

That got me curious. Had they told me they were making dirty jokes or sitting around passing egg yolks from mouth to mouth, I would have gone to bed.

"I knew your mother in college," the taller woman said.

"You went to college?" I asked.

"Of course!" she said, laughing.

"How did you know her?"

"We were in the student organization together. She was a big deal."

"Oh," I said.

"You mother was a big shot," the smaller woman said. "An organizer. For student demonstrations."

"Really?"

"Yeah," the taller woman said. "We had a couple of big protests, and the police were crawling up the walls to get her."

"Why?"

"Because she was part of the student organization."

"Was that illegal?"

"It was if you were for democracy," Mr. Kang said.

"Or if you were against the president," the taller woman said.

"But she was in college during Park Chung-hee's presidency," I said.

"That's right," Mr. Kang said.

"Did she eat a flag?" the taller woman asked Abeoji.

"*Aye-shh*!" he said.

"Why would they arrest her for supporting Park Chung-hee?" I said. "Omoni loves Park Chung-hee."

The four of them quieted, and the bed of coals snapped. "Because she didn't support Park Chung-hee," the taller woman said. "Your mother *hated* Park Chung-hee. She hated Chun Doo-whan, too. She hated all of them."

"That's not true," I told them. "She even has a picture on the wall of President Park."

"Exactly," the taller woman said. "Why do you think she is so determined to prove her allegiance?"

"Do you know what they would have done to her if they had caught her?" Mr. Kang asked me. "You do not want to know."

"Whatever happened, happened for a reason," Abeoji said.

"What time is it?" I said.

"They would have started by raping her," Mr. Kang said.

"It's bedtime," Abeoji said.

"Shouldn't we be headed home?" I asked Abeoji.

"Tell him what you heard on the news this morning," Mr. Kang said to the taller woman.

"It's not important," she said.

"Go on," Mr. Kang said.

"They found your boat," she said.

My bowels cooled.

"That's not all," Mr. Kang said. "It gets better."

"It turns out," she said, "the police claim that the boat was stolen by North Korean infiltrators. But due to the gross ineptitude of the infiltrators, they crashed the boat, and they escaped."

"They're still on the loose," Abeoji said.

Mr. Kang winked at me.

"Good thing we weren't on the boat when it happened," Abeoji said.

"They could have killed you," the shorter woman said, sitting next to Mr. Kang. I had never seen a woman sitting as close to Mr. Kang as the shorter woman sat. In fact, I had never seen him sit with a woman, ever. And the taller woman sat so close to Abeoji you would have thought they were married. Had I ever seen Abeoji and Omoni sit close together, hold hands or show any public affection?

"They *would* have killed you," the taller woman said.

"These weren't regular North Koreans," Abeoji said. "They were trained killers."

"They have no concept of life," the tall woman said. "Like living robots. I wouldn't be surprised if they weren't cannibals."

"I hear they smell different," the smaller woman said, gold tooth. "They're food has changed over the years, and they have a stink to them."

"Well, we are here now," Mr. Kang said. "A close call, indeed."

"Hopefully, they don't see the fire and decide to get us here," Abeoji said, pinching the woman's ribs. "Help themselves to a free meal."

"Stop!" the tall woman said, and each of the women scooted closer to the men.

"The truth is," Mr. Kang said, "whether they come here tonight or not is all up to fate. The question is, what have you done with your life, and have you spent your time wisely? Have you accomplished your desires and goals that make this nightmare worthwhile? That is the question. That is the only question! Are you happy with how you have spent your time? Are you even *satisfied*?"

"No," Abeoji said. "I never wanted this life."

Maybe my father had drunk so much that day and *evening* that he had forgotten about my presence, that I was standing there observing the entire conversation, even though I had participated in the conversation just minutes before. In a moment, I realized that they *all* had forgotten about me. I could have walked away, but they had turned into reptilian people, where any movement would catch their attention. Forced to remain silent and still, I endured the conversation.

"I never even wanted children," Abeoji said, "but it

happens to you, or it doesn't. It's like there is no rhyme or reason."

"He's a good kid," the taller woman said, and the shorter woman agreed. "You're lucky," they both said.

"And your daughter is going to be a doctor," Mr. Kang reminded him.

"True," Abeoji said. "It could have been much worse."

"I say that's nonsense," Mr. Kang said. "You're a fool to say that you have wasted your life. What are you?"

"A failure," Abeoji said. "I married the wrong woman, had the wrong children and chose the wrong profession."

"A *fisherman*," Mr. Kang said. "There are very few men who can honestly contribute to society with their line of work. Name a profession that is both honest and fulfilling."

"Easy," Abeoji said. "Baseball players."

"*Besides* baseball," Mr. Kang said.

"Lawyers," Abeoji said.

"Listen to yourself talk!" Mr. Kang said, pulling the bottle of soju away from my father. "He has had enough," Mr. Kang said to the women. "Lawyers?"

That fast, the bottle was back in Abeoji's hands.

Mr. Kang continued. "Lawyers are concerned with whether or not they win or lose a case. They are not concerned with the truth. They use invisible words and boundaries, theorems and postulations to move power into their favor, money into their hands. Lawyers are just criminals with nice clothes."

"Okay," Abeoji said, "doctors."

"Doctors?" Mr. Kang said. "Who am I drinking with? You think well of these men who believe they can change the course of God's will with medicine and procedures? Nonsense. Doctors are worse than lawyers. At least lawyers know that they are evil. Doctors have convinced themselves that they are working for the good of mankind, and all they do is treat us like Guinea pigs. And then they have the nerve to charge money. Let me get this straight, if you have enough money, then a doctor will cure you. If not, then you are left to die. Now he is playing God twice!"

"You've never been to the doctor?" the short woman said.

"Of course, I have. That's why I can say this," Mr. Kang said.

"What about carpenters?" the tall woman said.

"Carpenters are the same as doctors, only they build with materials instead of humans. They build structures that break down, and usually, on purpose. They want you to call them back for repairs. They cheat you with materials. You know what happens when I cheat you with bait? You don't catch fish—I don't get paid. You know what happens when a carpenter cheats you and your house breaks down? You call him back and he gets more work. In other words, he gets a bonus!"

"Why don't you just call a different carpenter?" the short woman said.

"Because they are all the same," Mr. Kang said.

"Stockbrokers," the tall woman said.

"Stockbrokers are just fortune tellers," Mr. Kang said.

"Writers?"

"*Propagandists!*"

"Teachers," the short woman said.

"Liars," Mr. Kang said. "And thieves."

"Painters," Abeoji said, and it sounded as if his voice came from the woods. Mr. Kang quieted, and the short woman slipped her arm inside his.

Mr. Kang lowered his head, then closed his eyes. Mr.

Kang was so drunk that I got the spins just watching him. "Painters are prostitutes," he said. "What do they do? They play with paint and colors, please themselves when others are pleased. They are emotionally needy and unhappy unless they are under the spell of the adulation of fools. Do painters, themselves, have any idea whatsoever whether the work they complete is perfection or garbage?"

"Even Seong?" Abeoji said.

"Especially, Seong," Mr. Kang said. "But that doesn't mean I don't love the boy. He has to find his way, and until he does, then he is just a prostitute. He is already addicted to the money. You saw the clothes he wore to tell us he was leaving. You saw his paintings, too. Pictures of animals with abstract doo-dahs and images and Greek statues."

"So?" the smaller woman said.

"So," Mr. Kang said, "Why does Seong paint pictures of the ancient Greeks? Who are they to him? What have the Greeks done to his life besides establish a standard that has nothing to do with Seong, himself, his way of life, ancestry or culture? They are two different worlds, and why does he defer to a culture that does not belong to him?"

My God, I had never heard Mr. Kang speak like this. Standing there, feeling both betrayed and fascinated all at once.

"But you are a painter," Abeoji said.

"*Was* a painter," Mr. Kang said. "I *was* a painter. But I was never a prostitute. I painted portraits of a leader I believed in and was, in fact, working for the people. Fine—you want to escape poverty and humiliation, then you have to work for it! You can't work eight-hour days. You can't even work ten-hour days. You have to work *all* day. You work all day and maybe you have a chance, but without the effort, you are a nobody. So yes, I painted pictures of a man whom I felt had pulled our country together, and when he and his henchmen, his robots, burned my pictures, I never painted an image since, and I turned to the only profession out there that is honorable—fishing."

"I'd like to be a doctor," the shorter woman said.

"Criminals," Mr. Kang said. "All of them."

"I don't think so," she said.

I tried to step backward, but the branches cracked beneath my feet. They all looked briefly my direction. Maybe the fire caused the glare to render me invisible, but I stood still.

"Who benefits directly from the work of fishermen?" Mr. Kang said.

"The fisherman," Abeoji said. "He gets paid."

"No," Mr. Kang said. "The hungry. Us. The people. Sure, the fisherman gets paid, but only a small portion for the goods delivered and the expertise involved. The expertise, by the way, he must acquire on his own, which requires a lifetime of practice, with no guarantee of success."

"True," the taller woman said, squeezing Abeoji's arm.

"The fisherman delivers a fish that the hungry desire. Fishermen must deliver these specific fish, and this system controls the quality. See, no fisherman takes pride in catching catfish. We catch croaker, snapper, mackerel, and delight in the joy of those who crave protein in this fashion. We catch fish at depths appropriate for eating raw. And how do we get these fish? Through our own specific expertise. That's how, and it is incorruptible."

"Nothing is incorruptible," the short woman said.

"Yes, it is," Mr. Kang said. "Corruption doesn't work with fishing."

"Bribery works," Abeoji said.

"How can you say that?" Mr. Kang said.

"You can bribe officials for fishing rights."

"You can, but you will ruin the fishing. Therefore, bribery doesn't work. Neither does nepotism or cronyism. None of that works unless those who you hire to fish have the gift, and if they do have the gift, then it isn't corrupt. Fish do not magically jump into your net or bite your lure. You don't even have to know how you do it. You just need the gift."

"He's right," the taller woman said.

"What about you?" Abeoji said to Mr. Kang. "I hired you, and we are friends."

"We are friends because we respected each other's ability to fish. You hired me because of my craft. And I accepted the job because I could fish on the job, and you wouldn't fire me for it. The relationship was purely transactional. Eventually, of course, we had many things in common. I had no family—you never wanted a family. We both liked to fish, thus we got along, like people do, and you performed a job that I could respect, unlike all the others—bankers, cops, insurance mongers, real estate crooks, stockbrokers, *soldiers*. You were the first person who made sense after I realized that the life I had led before was a lie." Mr. Kang paused to take a drink. "Take your son. You think your son can be a good fisherman just because his father is a master? Even the son of a master fisherman is lousy unless he has the gift."

"Aye-shhh," Abeoji said.

"Wait," gold tooth said. "We've been eating the fish that his son caught."

"That's right. And he caught the fish because he has been out here figuring it out, not because he is the son of a fisherman. Though, I grant you, he can't even drive a boat."

The shorter woman giggled.

"My god. Do not let the boy near a boat," Mr. Kang said.

"Straight into the tetrapods?" Abeoji said.

"That's right," Mr. Kang said.

"He did not," the taller woman said.

Mr. Kang talked with his hands, telling and showing the other three how the boat almost sailed into the air, accelerating and literally jumping onto the tetrapods, as if I were trying to drive through them.

The women laughed, and the taller woman said I could have died.

"He's worthless," Abeoji said.

"That's not true," the tall woman said.

"It is true," he said.

"You should have seen him," Mr. Kang said. "I had to breathe into him, and he must have been dreaming. He put his arms around my head. He must have thought I was a mermaid. He even moaned when he said, 'I love you.'"

Slowly, I bent down towards the ground, feeling with my hand some solid ground to brace myself. Abeoji stood and dropped a couple logs onto the fire. Coals and sparks erupted in a plume, creating enough of a racket for me to sit down completely and eventually close my eyes and listen to them talk. What other choice did I have?

"Listen," Mr. Kang said, "all of us wish we could have done more with our lives."

I fell asleep. Again, the pigs appeared. This time, I rose and looked out at the water from the top of a tree, and it occurred to me, during my slumber, that I could fly, and it was as easy as stretching out my arms, but beneath me was not the water, nor the formations under the water, or even the ground, but a sea of pigs, swarming all over each other, pressing their bodies against one another, stepping on each other and creating a sea of swine misery. The pigs sometimes looked directly at me, and their wet snouts glistened in the moonlight. The sound of their misery sickened me, and even in my dream state I thought I might vomit, my stomach filled with hot sand, and I did vomit in my dream, continuing to vomit all over the pigs beneath me, and it wasn't until I lost the ability to fly and swooned toward the ground and disappeared into the sea of pigs that I awoke with a start. To my surprise, somebody, presumably one of the women, had covered me with a blanket and placed an empty bottle of Munhak under my head for a pillow.

XXVI

The bed of coals continued to shimmer, the logs of driftwood and pine fully digested by the flames. I added more branches and logs, the flames taking them in greedily, the sight of it awakening my own hunger, and I bit into an orange and devoured several steamed buns, which had dried and toughened in the air. The grown-ups were absent from the platform. My stomach cooled for a moment, with the possibility that they had forgotten about me so thoroughly that they had left without me. I whispered their names but heard nothing in return. In the moonlight, I could see the granite path that descended to the beachhead in one direction and Mr. Kang's dingy in the opposite direction. I stepped carefully to avoid breaking my ankles and becoming incapacitated on the island if they had left, or further burdening them if they were still on the island, wherever they were.

An irrational thought occurred to me that my recurring dreams of pigs had been, in fact, warnings, and that just as snakes had found their way to the island, perhaps pigs had as well, and this unlikely fate lay waiting for me. All I knew was, the faster I got to the beachhead, the better. I could sleep on the sand, and nothing could bother me, unless the tide came in, and then the water would waken me softly, thoughtfully, creeping up slowly to let me know it was time to get moving for the day. The last thing I wanted was to remain at the platform and listen to Abeoji and Mr. Kang, or the women, whoever they were. I slid my feet forward, engaging in a modified walk and slide hybrid action, keeping the weight of my body at an angle, my center of gravity steady. But of course, I was walking myself to my own demise. I knew this—I could hear the digging and foraging of animals. I had seen the ground dug up by pigs on Geoje (also an island, also rich with swine!), and the sound ahead created images in my mind of this action. Continuing to walk slowly, another thought occurred to me that I could find the dwelling place of these pigs and set a future trap. What a way to prove to Abeoji and his friends that I did have something to offer by showing up to camp one morning with a slaughtered pig cooking over the fire!

The presence of these animals on the island terrified me, but why else would I have been in this position if this were not my fate? The island, the dreams? No, this was not true at all. I knew what was making this sound when I heard the laughter of the women below. Mr. Kang and Abeoji had caught a pig, and they were in the process of a slaughter themselves. Both of the women laughed so loudly, I thought perhaps maybe one of them had been attacked by the pig itself, and as the moon emerged from behind the clouds, I quickened my pace and made my way down the granite trail, the surface of the rock embedded into my memory more than I had given it credit for, reaching the opening to the beach where blackened areas on the beach appeared with bodies on each, the bodies moving in utter chaos and violence, legs writhing and heads bobbing, arms so long, whitening streams of flesh on the fabric, the combination of sounds—anger, joy and panic, ggool-ggool, all at once. I stepped on a branch of dried driftwood, and the snap broke the evening in half, and the figures writhing on the mat stopped, and perhaps it is only my memory revising the scene, but a gold tooth reflected white against the moonlight. "Punk," I heard a voice say.

The skies clear with the moon shining down on the path, I sprinted up the granite hill to the campsite. I looked for any semblance of bedding, other than my own soju bottle pillow.

To be honest, I had no desire to wait until daybreak to leave the island, and I had no desire to steal Mr. Kang's boat and steer the dingy home, feeding their lust for humiliation. Nor did I have the desire to wait at home and suffer the consequences for leaving my father behind, should I show up at the Jisepo docks and take the 67-1 bus home. *Why did you leave your father with that animal*? Omoni would ask. First the shouting, then the cane. Forget that. Instead, I stood above the small cliff next to the boat where I had explored the depths for oyster. I knew what was down there. Down there was nothing. Not a goddamned thing but rock face and barnacles. Why should I wait until daybreak to leave? I pulled the shirt over my torso and dropped it on the ground. Diving headfirst, the granite surface left my feet and gravity took me downwards, accelerating until my fingertips cut through the surface, the water punching my forehead, and silence overtaking me until I once again found the air and took a breath. I looked south at the line of lights on the horizon—fishing boats in the distance, and then I turned north. I aimed for the lights of Nambu and started swimming.

Why not? For all I knew, Abeoji and Mr. Kang had decided to stay on the island for good.

Tɪᴍ Fɪᴛᴛs is the author of two short story collections, *Hypothermia* (Madhat Press 2017) and *Go Home and Cry for Yourselves* (Xavier Review Press 2017). His novel, *The Soju Club*, (Loupe 2016), was published in Korea as a Korean translation. His short stories have been featured in journals such as Granta, Boulevard, The Gettysburg Review, AXT, The Baltimore Review, among others. Fitts teaches in the Liberal Arts Department of The Curtis Institute of Music, is also a songwriter for the group, *Delray Banks and the Prophets*, and is currently collaborating with composer Thomas Weaver for his collection of prose poems, *American Jackal*, coming in 2025 from Madhat Press.

9 781963 908138